# HOW TO HEAL A GRYPHON

# HOW TO HEAL A GRYPHON

## MEG CANNISTRA

inkyard
PRESS

Recycling programs for this product may not exist in your area.

For my familiars: Gloom, Doom, Fester, and Anthony Jr.

And to Coconut, Kiwi, Blackjack, Ooh La La, Coalie, and Maple.

**1**

It's not my fault I'm late. But when you're a guaritrice-in-training, you can't be tardy. No excuses.

You can't leave your shirt untucked or have a single hair on your head out of place. You can't be too loud or talk back. Most importantly, though, you can't use your powers for anything but helping people.

Even if being a guaritrice doesn't interest you at all.

I push the sweaty curls from my forehead, struggling to bike up the winding cobblestone road that leads to the tallest tower in all of the Amalfi Coast. Guaritori-in-training aren't allowed to sweat, either. At least that's what my brother,

Rocco, claims. Not that I actually believe him or anything. *Everyone* sweats.

The church bells chime the hour just as the road becomes level and the blue-green sea peeks out from underneath the cliff side. The salty air hits my face, and I take a big deep breath, filling my lungs with the sweet sea breeze. I stand on my pedals and glide alongside the cliff. My backpack wriggles in the handlebar basket, a small squeak escaping it.

"Shhh, little one. You'll be home soon." I pedal faster, feeling sorry about the cooped-up creature. But my backpack was the only place I could think to hide her for now. "Once class is over."

The Torre di Apollo sprouts up from the cliff like a sunflower. An impossibly tall tower cutting straight through the sky and kissing the clouds. Bougainvillea crawls up its side, the bright magenta flowers exploding color against the creamy sandstone.

I take a right, flying past tufts of wild lavender and groups of tourists snapping pictures at the tower's base.

"Slow down, Giada," Signora Alfonsi calls as she collects flowers to make into soaps and lotions for her shop. "You're going to break your neck!"

But I don't listen. I've never fallen in my life. But if I did, my family could fix a broken bone with their ossa rotte, thick as the best sauce and guaranteed to mend even the worst fracture. Signora Alfonsi knows that, but it doesn't stop her from fussing every time I fly by her on my bike.

I dodge a bunch of people with nosy cameras. Christmas is one of the busiest times of the year. Tourists love the Amalfi Coast, even if most of them don't know the full truth like everyone who lives here. For non-streghe, the stories about healers and magic are myths. Fairy tales you read in children's books. It's easier that way. If they knew magic was real—that guaritori really can cast out the fantasmi causing your migraines or remove the balding curse from your husband's head—we'd never be able to get anything done. It'd be more crowded than it already is. All the people trampling in from all over the world to take in more than just good Italian food and the sites. It could be dangerous, too. With people even forcing us to use our magic. And we can't have that. Not that we don't want to help people. We do. It's just easier for us to do it quietly and behind the scenes, when we have time to create the best potions and spells possible.

I make my way to the back of the tower—the *real* entrance. I snatch my backpack from the basket, making sure I'm careful not to jostle it too much, before hopping from my bike and leaving it in the grass.

"Late again, Giada?" Signor Stefano, one of the Torre di Apollo's guards, says. He's posing with an American woman wearing a fanny pack while a man in cargo shorts takes their picture. They stand next to one of the big Christmas trees Signor Stefano and the other guards put up last week. All of the tower's guards dress in long white robes, gold sandals, and laurel wreaths. Like the gladiators with plastic armor and swords that stand outside the Colosseum. A disguise so the tourists aren't alarmed by how many guards are patrolling.

"I'm sure the first ten minutes went fine without me," I call back.

Signor Stefano laughs. "Maestra Vita might think otherwise."

I yank open the heavy oak door and hurry down a long hallway where another oak door stands. This one has a special lock that can only be opened by the guaritore crest, a laurel wreath with a raven's head in the middle. I pull a necklace from a pocket on my backpack and press the pendant into the lock. The lock glows, the door creaking open an inch.

I barrel through and take the spiral stone steps two at a time, all the way up to the thirteenth floor. The stairwell walls are painted a crisp pure white. Hundreds of glittering lucciole dip and dive between portraits of famous guaritori. Their bright wings fluttering and flickering.

So many of my ancestors stare down at me, the Bellantuonos being the most well-known of the strega families in all of Italy. Papa's up there and so is my bisnonna. Rocco expects his picture to be on the wall by the time he turns eighteen. Which is a little ambitious, if you ask me. No guaritore has ever made the wall before their thirtieth birthday.

There's no way they'll ever put my face up there. I don't want to follow Apollo and heal *people* like all the other guaritori. It's not part of my plan.

I pause on the step in front of Papa's portrait. His unblinking eyes are creepy and don't have any of the warmth his real ones do. I take a deep breath. I have to tell him tonight that I want to honor Diana, goddess of wild animals, and take care of creatures—both ordinary and extraordinary. Worry twists around my heart, but I tear my gaze away from his portrait and hurry up to class.

After a few more stairs, I reach a small landing and dart to a silver door emblazoned with a gold python wrapped around a glimmering lyre. I catch my breath, wiping my forehead with the back of my arm. I take a whiff of my armpit. Yuck. I smell like a whole red onion. Hopefully no one will get close enough to smell me.

My backpack bumps against my back.

*Chirrup, chirrup, chirrup.*

"You gotta be quiet for a bit, okay?" I whisper to my backpack, slipping my fingers underneath the flap and tickling a soft feathered head. "Only a little while longer." The small creature grows quiet. I pat down the loose strands of hair that fell out of my braid and rub the gold cornicello hanging from my neck. Preparing myself for Maestra Vita.

She's standing at the front of the class with the blackboard at her side. Maestra Vita's a tall woman with long brown hair she sweeps into a tight bun at the back of her head. Black-rimmed glasses are always perched on her sloping nose. It's rare to see her in anything other than a white dress of some sort. Most of the kids in my school are scared of her, so she teaches the graduating guaritore students for a reason. But she doesn't bother me too much and she's too busy answering a question to notice me. Yet.

"No, there's no restorative potion that can make a person taller. Nor is there one to grow back a limb that's long since deteriorated. This is standard stuff you should already know. It's going to be part of your oath ceremony." She starts pacing at the front of the classroom, hands behind her back. "There are limitations to our magic. We can't *cure* illnesses or maladies. We can't manipulate rooted traits like height. Our magic works alongside modern medicine and shouldn't be used as a substitute. What do we always say?"

The class choruses: "We don't cure, we strengthen."

"That's right," she confirms. "We can take a moment to review ingredients for the recipe again. Your families will have their own methods for brewing restorative potions, of course, but the basic ingredients are very similar."

Maestra Vita takes up a nub of chalk and starts writing on the blackboard. "As you learned way back in your first year of formal training, lizard tail is perhaps one of the most versatile ingredients. Key to fertility balms and tinctures to mend a broken bone, it even helps with balding."

Pens scratch quickly against paper, catching her every word. I duck behind the back row and tiptoe to my seat.

"Don't think I can't see you." I pop up from my hiding spot on the other side of an empty desk to find her staring straight at me, arms crossed over her chest and eyebrows raised to her hairline. "You're not as stealthy as you think you are."

"Nothing escapes you now that you've got new glasses, Maestra Vita. They look great, by the way." I smile brightly, but she doesn't return it.

Finally, she pushes her glasses up the bridge of her white nose and waves a hand. "Sit down, Giada. We're reviewing restorative healing."

I sigh. More of the same stuff.

Lessons and apprenticeships are boring when you've already done what's being taught. Mamma and Papa let me work with Rocco before taking the official oath, which kind of goes against the rules. No other family lets their children help out with real healing work until after they turn thirteen and pledge to carry on the tradition. The Bellantuonos—being as renowned as we are—get a pass on some things.

It's supposed to be homeschooling until nine, then

formal lessons for four years, going through each year with guaritore kids your age. Right after that, you have a yearlong apprenticeship with a guaritore family in a completely different part of the world. But while it's nice being able to help people have babies or ease aches and pains, that's not at all how I want to use my magic.

Rocco was born to be a guaritore. Our papa and mamma couldn't be prouder. He honors Apollo. He's calm and plays by the rules. He listens to patients when they go on and on about their symptoms and all the research they did online. He doesn't get annoyed when patients insist we can cure colds or set a bone with a snap of our fingers. I, on the other hand, get huffy when patients question me or act like they know better than me. Papa says I have the bedside manner of a two-headed toad, which I think is awesome. But my family doesn't.

I slink to my seat and put my backpack on the big dark wooden desk I share with Alessia Marini. She's already thirteen and thinks that means she's wiser than me. A know-it-all. And also my best friend. It's always been Giada and Alessia, Alessia and Giada. Which makes sense since we're two of only a handful of students our age who live in Positano year-round. Most of my schoolmates come from other cities to train and live in the Torre di Apollo just for the school year.

Alessia ruffles her short curly brown hair with her fingers, her wide hazel eyes set on the sweat stains on my blouse. "I waited for you outside your house, but I couldn't wait *forever*," she whispers. "You were taking sooo long that I was worried I'd grow gray hairs before you were ready to leave."

"I'll bring you some of my papa's Capelli Grigi potion next time. It'll keep the brown strands from turning." I roll my eyes. "And I was busy." I smile, carefully pulling my notebook and pen from my backpack without disturbing the little bambina inside.

Her eyebrows knit together. "Busy doing what?"

"So what did I miss?" I ask, ignoring her question. "Can I copy your notes?"

"Later."

Maestra Vita has written *onions*, *mountain air*, and *fat from a black hen* underneath *lizard tails* on the blackboard. "Let's get more specific. What ingredients could be used in a fertility elixir where the parents wish for only one child? Yes, Marco."

Marco puts his hand down and leans forward in his seat to answer Maestra Vita's question. "Fruit of the mandrake."

"Yes, but remember to use extreme caution and only pluck the fruit. If you dig up the plant, the mandrake will produce an ear-piercing scream that will kill you. Let us not forget about what happened to Paolo and Maria Abbadellis."

Quiet falls over the room. Every guaritore uses Paolo and Maria's fatal mandrake expedition as a cautionary tale of just how dangerous our work can be.

Maestra Vita breaks the silence by writing *fruit of the mandrake* on the blackboard. "What else? You need to know this. Your ceremony's less than two weeks away. Christmas Eve is fast approaching," she reminds us, her back still turned to us. "Fruit of the mandrake is good, but it works in all fertility spells. Give me something specific to only *one* child."

"Ground saltwater pearl," Alessia says.

"Very good. An oyster only produces one pearl at a time. Procure a fresh saltwater pearl and use a marble mortar and pestle to crush it until smooth. What else?"

*Chirrup, chirrup.*

My stomach jumps into my throat. I sneak a hand underneath my backpack's flap to try to calm the little creature.

"What was that?" Maestra Vita asks, chalk pausing against the blackboard. The class is silent. A few kids look for the source of the noise. "Did someone say something?" She turns around, eyes scanning the room for a hand.

*Chirrup, chirrup, chirrup.*

Alessia eyes my backpack and gives me a funny look.

"Your bag's moving."

I put a hand on top of my backpack to stop it from squirming across the desk. "No, it's not."

"Because you're holding on to it now."

"Something the matter, Giada?" Maestra Vita asks, eyebrows arched. The whole class turns to face me.

"Not at all." I straighten my shoulders, hand firmly on top of my backpack. "Just trying to find my notebook."

"Isn't that it right in front of you?" She nods to the unicorn-emblazoned notebook sitting in front of me.

"Ha, uhh, you're right."

*Chirrup, chirrup.*

"Giada?"

"Yes?"

"Is your backpack chirping?"

*Chirrup, chirrup, chirrup.*

"No…"

*Chirrup, chirrup!*

Before I can stop her, the creature wiggles out from my backpack and flutters unsteadily to perch on me. I try to pull her down, but she holds tight, digging her talons into my hair, her back paws balancing on my shoulder. She flaps her fuzzy wings, her furry lion-like tail wrapping around my neck.

"Giada Bellantuono!" Maestra Vita shouts. Her voice echoes through the stone room before bouncing against my eardrums. "Were you hiding a baby gryphon in your backpack?"

"I wasn't *hiding* her exactly. She could've come out at any time, but I knew you wouldn't like that."

Maestra Vita clenches her teeth so hard she might grind them to dust. "Why do you have this gryphon?"

"I found her fending for herself on the way home from lessons last week. I nursed her back to health."

"You nursed her back to health?" She purses her lips.

"She was hurting." I shrug. "Of course I helped her."

"You used your magic?" Maestra Vita pinches the bridge of her nose. She always says out of all her students, I give

**19**

her the most headaches. I expect today is no exception. "You're a guaritrice, Giada. You can only use your magic to heal *people*."

"Technically, I'm only training to be a guaritrice. And maybe there should be other guaritori who take care of creatures. It's completely missing from our tradition. Don't you think?" The gryphon—who I've been calling Piccolina since last Tuesday—plucks at my hair with her beak.

"It's simply the way things are."

"Well, that's not very nice."

Piccolina chirps loudly. She leaps from my head and flaps her wings furiously, getting a few feet into the air before tumbling back onto the desk with a loud thud. A few kids start laughing and others gasp.

"Why are you like this?" Isabella asks, turning all the way around in her seat to get a better look. A mean sneer spreads over her freckled face. "This is so mortifying."

Alessia buries her head in her hands, ears pink with humiliation. "Giada!"

I scoop Piccolina off the desk and set her back on my shoulder. "Well, I'm not mortified."

"Leave, Giada!" Maestra Vita bellows. The class quiets, backs straightening, attention on the front of the room.

"You've distracted us enough for one day. I'll be calling your father this evening."

My eyes widen as her words weigh down on me like a boulder. I squeeze my cornicello. "Please don't, Maestra Vita! Papa won't be happy with me," I beg, my voice soft. Isabella and a couple others snicker, hiding their smiles behind their hands.

"You should have thought of that before causing trouble." She shakes her head. "Your brother would never behave this way. Rocco was my best student. If only you were more like him."

Heat rises to my face. I grab my backpack and stomp toward the door. "He's not all that great, you know."

Before Maestra Vita can say anything else about my amazing big brother, I slam the door behind me, thumping loudly down the stairs.

**2**

Piccolina nuzzles her head into the crook of my neck as I carry her up the steep twisting stone stairs carved into the rocky part of the tallest cliff. No tourist would ever dare climb all the way up here, but it's the perfect spot for a mamma gryphon to hunt for food.

"It's gonna be okay," I whisper against Piccolina's fluffy down feathers. She kneads her paws into my shoulder. "Your mamma's got to be around here somewhere."

My stomach churns as Maestra Vita's angry face bubbles up in my memories like the chunks of veal in osso buco.

Her words echo in my ears and beat alongside Isabella's question: *Why are you like this?*

I don't know how else to be. I wish I had yelled it. I wish I had been able to write it in the biggest, most humongous letters on the board.

What she probably really meant was: *Why aren't you more like your famous brother, Rocco?*

I'll never manage to crawl out from under Rocco's shadow. He's only sixteen and already on his way to being one of the most famous fixers ever.

I grit my teeth, hugging Piccolina closer.

"There's nothing wrong with me." I know this for a fact because I know I'm not the only nontraditional guaritrice out there. My pen pal, Moss Calamoneri, his dad uses music therapy to help heal people.

*Chirrup, chirrup!*

"You said it." I kick a rock off the stairs, and it hurtles all the way down to the sandy beach below. Most people hate heights, but when you live in Positano, the vertical city, climbing all the way up the side of a cliff is part of daily life. No matter how much you sweat. No matter how bad your thighs rub together. You can't get around it. So up, up, up I go.

We finally reach the top after 1,927 stairs. I once read a book that said the Empire State Building in New York City has 1,576 stairs and that every year people compete to see who can climb up the fastest. After I learned that, I started counting all the steps I climb every day. Outside of the Torre di Apollo's 3,288 steps, these 1,927 stairs are the most in all of Positano.

I balance Piccolina in one arm and pull my metal bottle from my backpack, gulping water so fast it dribbles down my chin.

*Chirrup, chirrup, chirrup!* Piccolina nips at my sleeve. She looks at me with wide black eyes, head tilted. I pour water into the cap of my bottle, and Piccolina pecks at it. I scratch the soft fur between her shoulder blades as she drinks. Her tail curls up around her backside, and she settles into my lap and spreads out across my round belly.

We look out on the small city together. The only place I've ever lived or been. Mamma says Amalfi is a magnet. Not like the ones on the fridge, but more like the ones that can pull things to it. Magical things. Like gryphons and mermaids and streghe. We have a map on the living room wall in our house of other regions like northern New Jersey, where the unicorns live, or the Kunlun Mountains in Tibet and China, where the phoenixes hide away. These regions tend to have easier access to ingredients and things like that, too. All the magic concentrated in one place is why so many guaritori kids come to Positano to study. And why our apprenticeships are usually in other magical regions across the world.

Papa said because Positano had innate magical properties and was much quieter, many magic users came here to hide centuries ago and fantastical beings migrated here for safety. To get away from the busyness of places like Tokyo or Athens or Paris or Cairo or Buenos Aires or Accra. Still, it's not as if they're good at lying low. After all, it's hard finding a good hiding spot if you're a gryphon with a wingspan as long as a car. The visitors coming to Positano often are so mesmerized by the guaritore lore that they don't pay the creatures much mind. Plus, most of the creatures have adapted and learned how to conceal themselves with either mirage spells or invisibility charms. If someone does focus enough to see through one of these spells or charms, most shrug the creatures off as the occasional ugly bird or weird-looking dolphin. That's easier to explain away than a Harpy or hippocampus.

Carefully, so as not to bother Piccolina, I scoot my backpack closer and pull out a pencil and my vet's log—a dragon scale journal filled with my renderings and research. Piccolina yawns, stretching out her legs, and we look up at a bright and clear sky.

"It'll be cold soon, Piccolina," I say, flipping my log open to a clean page, dating it, and beginning a sketch of a tiny baby gryphon sitting atop a tall cliff. "I won't get to do this anymore."

Cold weather means more work for healers because it's flu season. The time of year people need us the most. They even ruin Christmas with all their needs.

"The meeting is coming up. All the heads of the guaritore families will come to my house to organize the apprenticeships for those who turned thirteen and finished their lessons. Mamma's going to give me a thousand things to do. I won't be able to hide up here anymore."

*Chirrup, chirrup, chirrup!*

"Totally unfair, right?" I ruffle her head. "Rocco didn't have to do an apprenticeship because they started after he became a guaritore. So why should I?"

She nuzzles me. *Chirrup, chirrup, chirrup!*

"I don't want to go live with another family. It's for a whole year. Can you imagine? What if someone's house

**26**

smells like three-day-old fish left out? Or stinky soup? You wouldn't want to live in a bad nest, right? Or one you didn't know?"

She blinks.

"It'll be all 'apply the ointment like this' and 'say the spell like that' and threats about not being able to moon beckon. Ugh!" It all swirls around in my stomach. I stab the air with my pencil. My thirteenth birthday is only a week away. I stare into her deep black eyes. "I've never been away from home before."

A whole year sleeping in a different family's house, eating a different family's dinners, and following a different family's rules feels like it's going to be the worst thing to ever happen to me. I already have trouble following my own family's. So many of them are based around old superstitions most streghe believe in. Like when you spill salt, you're supposed to toss it over your left shoulder so you don't get bad luck. Or how we wear the cornicello for all kinds of protection, but mainly against the malocchio, which some also call the evil eye.

It's not that I don't believe in any of it—I do, I've seen bad luck with my own eyes—but all the rules feel like wearing an itchy wool sweater in the middle of summer.

Superstitions make people scared. Too scared to be brave. And I don't like being scared.

Maybe it'll all work out when I tell Papa I don't want to heal people. Maybe he'll be understanding and will even let me push off my apprenticeship at least another year. But the chances of that are slimmer than a crescent moon.

*Chirrup, chirrup, chirrup!*

"What's up, Piccolina?" I ask. "More water?"

*Chirrup!*

*Screech!*

A louder, deeper bird call cuts through the air. Piccolina's on her feet, prancing behind me.

I sit up and turn around, eyes widening. My vet's log and pencil fall from my hands.

A humongous—at least six hundred pounds—gryphon slowly paces only a few feet away, her wings spread wide and glimmering in the sun. She pauses for a moment before nodding over to Piccolina. The little gryphon chirps loudly in response. Revving up her hind legs, Piccolina flutters toward her mamma and leaps onto her back.

*Screech, screech!*

*Chirrup, chirrup, chirrup!*

Mamma Gryphon limps across the cliff, her left back

paw dragging behind her. She winces, and Piccolina slides down off her back.

Something's wrong.

On her leg is an open wound nearly four inches long. Old blood crusts the fur around the gash. She picks at it and calls out again, a painful shriek that sends shivers down my spine. I walk toward her on my tiptoes.

Mamma Gryphon looks up. She wraps a protective wing over Piccolina and narrows her eyes at me.

"I'm not gonna hurt you." I put my hands out before me. My heart beats so loud I can hardly hear my own voice. She's about five times my size and could easily snatch me up by the collar and fling me off the side of the cliff. "I wanna help you feel better. Like I did for your cub."

Piccolina trots out from underneath her and stands by my side as if she knows we need to convince her mamma. The little gryphon nuzzles my hand with her head. Telling her it's all right. That I can be trusted. I step back toward my backpack without breaking eye contact and sidle up next to her wounded leg.

Mamma Gryphon whips her head around. *Screech, screech, screeeeeech!* she warns.

I fall onto my butt. Soreness shoots through my body. That'll be a bruise, even with all my extra cushioning.

"You can trust me," I manage to squeak out. "Please let me help you."

*Chirrup, chirrup.* Piccolina bounces next to us. Mamma Gryphon softens and extends her injured leg so I can get a better look.

It's worse than I thought. Pus congeals around the wound like rotten mascarpone. The gash is infected. It never would've healed on its own.

I open my guaritrice pack and remove two long strips of spider silk threaded with unicorn tail, a small bottle of pureed melon, and a jar of immortal jellyfish goo. "Here's what I'm gonna do," I inform Mamma Gryphon. I can feel my magic thrumming in my blood and bouncing off my vocal cords. She might not know the words I'm saying, but creatures understand. They sense magic. "Knowing the steps makes it easier."

She closes her eyes, chest rising and falling with deep breaths. I mix the pureed melon with rubbing alcohol and smear it on a piece of the silk, dabbing carefully at the wound. "Melon is perfect for topical wounds and great for your skin. It gets deep in there. Moisturizes, too. Some

**30**

ladies use it to stay pretty. And the rubbing alcohol cleans up all the blood and pus."

Mamma Gryphon cries out.

I place a gentle hand on her leg. "I know. It can sting, but it's working."

I open the jar of jellyfish goo and carefully apply it with a spoon made from olive wood. "Immortal jellyfish are supercool. They can morph from old to young and young to old whenever they please. Isn't that extraordinary?"

Piccolina cocks her head to the side. Her mamma says nothing in response.

I clear my throat. "Anyway, their goo—which we only collect when they wash ashore—is, like, the number one healing ingredient." I wrap the clean silk bandage over the wound and around her leg twice. Spider silk is tougher than any other material, and the unicorn hair will lessen the pain. Mamma Gryphon whimpers, but the sharp edge is gone.

I pull out one more jar from my backpack. A salve made from aloe vera, cocoa butter, hydra milk, and rose oil. I apply a thin layer to the skin around her bandage. "This is a salve I use all the time. It's antichafing and prevents discomfort. I invented it a couple years ago because my thighs rub together, which can hurt. Especially in the summer." After applying the salve, I put the jar away and scramble to my feet, dusting off my knees. "Two days tops, and you'll be good as new."

Mamma Gryphon opens her eyes and inspects the fresh bandage wrapped around her leg.

*Screech, screech!* She jumps up, a little unsteady at first, and trots around the top of the cliff. Piccolina races after her.

"You're doing great!" I clap my hands, cheering on the pair as they make another lap.

Mamma Gryphon comes to a stop before me and presses her forehead to mine. My magic buzzes through my body and pushes against my skin like a bee trapped in a glass jar, determined to get out. I rub the brilliant white feathers at her neck. She moves against my hand, letting me collect her stray feathers. They're oily and sturdy, perfect for flight. So different from Piccolina's soft baby feathers.

Happiness swells in my chest as she lets me take seven of her feathers. Gryphon feathers guard against dark magic and they're very rare. You should only take a gryphon's feathers if they let you. Sometimes, bad streghe will take them without permission, but if you do, they don't work. The magic seeps out of them.

Mamma Gryphon steps back and bows. I curtsy in return as Piccolina hops onto her mamma once more and nestles safely between her wings. Mamma Gryphon leaps into the air, flying toward the thick collection of trees about a mile north.

They soar through the sky, disappearing beyond a veil of thick green leaves. I watch until they're small dots.

I fight away the tiny twinge of sadness. I'll miss Piccolina. I miss every animal I get to help. Even though I'm not supposed to use guaritore spells and potions on them, I feel so much better after, like I'm a bone knocked out of its socket until I get to protect and nurse them.

The magic that vibrated in my body with such force starts to quiet, and my shoulders slump. Stowing away my vet's log and pencil, I make a mental note to jot down the exact steps I took to heal Mamma Gryphon when I get home. I pull an apple from the front pocket of my backpack and bite a huge chunk out of its side, following it with a long drink of water. Using magic, even the tiniest bit, takes energy. The first rule every strega learns, regardless of what kind of magic she practices, is to stay nourished. If you go overboard or forget to take care of yourself when using magic, you can pass out or even go into a coma.

I grab my backpack off the ground, put Mamma Gryphon's feathers carefully inside, and sling it over my shoulder. My stomach tightens. Maestra Vita probably called home after lessons. Papa now knows what I did. I don't regret it, but now I'll have to face the consequences. I hesitate at the top of the stairs, wondering if it's better to stay up here and hide for a few more hours.

My cornicello is heavy around my neck, and I rub the small horn between my fingers, trying to coax out any extra protection power. There's nothing bad about healing a baby gryphon with magic and helping her find her mamma. But this is at least the twenty-seventh time that I've been in trouble with Maestra Vita this year alone.

He's not going to be happy when I tell him about my plan. I can already picture his face turning as red as a pomodoro and the twitch in his jaw as I tell him. Mamma will try to keep the peace, but Papa will take it personally. His own daughter, going against the family tradition. I go to touch my cornicello again, but pause, fingers hovering just underneath the horn. "This isn't a bad-luck thing, Giada," I remind myself. "It's being brave. I can tell him."

With a small sigh, I start back down the 1,927 steps, trying not to think of his disappointment.

# 3

The front door opens before my hand even touches the knob.

"My sweet girl!" Zia Clementina exclaims. "It's been so long."

Before I can figure out what's happening, Zia Clementina wraps me in a hug. Her lavender perfume tickles my nose as she practically squeezes the life out of me.

"What are you doing here?" My voice is muffled against her shoulder.

Zia Clementina holds me at arm's length, inspecting me as if it's been years since we last saw each other and not just three months. She's my papa's younger sister and looks a lot like him, aside from being chubby like me and having a gold hoop nose ring in her left nostril. They've got the same brown eyes, thick dark eyebrows, and olive complexion.

Mamma says I'm their spitting image, but I'd say it's more a fifty-fifty split between them and her. Zia Clementina's a strega like the rest of us but isn't part of the "fixer" branch of magic like the guaritori. All people with magic like ours are streghe, but not all streghe are fixers. Fixers focus on magic that, well, fixes things. Guaritori focus on human medical magic, but fixer streghe can also work on things like magical architecture, magical transportation, and magical gardens. Non-fixers are part of other branches of magic and have special talents in areas such as alchemy, charms, or fortune-telling—like Zia Clementina. Regardless of what we do with our skills, we all come from the same tree of magical folk.

The differences aren't that major, but Papa would say otherwise. He, like a lot of streghe, see guaritori as the most important of the fixers because they heal people. Which is silly, if you ask me. How would we travel in a fraction of the time that non-streghe do if it weren't for magical mechanics? Or have a building as magnificent as the Torre di Apollo without the help of a magical architect? And, for Papa, non-fixer streghe are taken even less seriously. Not that he doesn't respect their magic, but he thinks guaritori are the most important and honorable. We almost never see Zia Clementina because she and Papa fight all the time about how she broke tradition and didn't take the oath to become a guaritrice.

"Your mamma called me this morning, and I got on the road soon after. She and your papa had to handle an emergency." She waves her hand through the air, ushering me inside and closing the door behind us.

My eyes widen. Zia Clementina's the best. Papa must be *really* desperate to have let her come take care of me and Rocco. Concern for Papa and Mamma and what they might be doing bubbles up but is immediately tamped back down by the realization that we'll have Zia Clementina staying here for at least a day or two.

I leave my backpack at the top of the large stone staircase and follow her down into the house. Ours is built into a cliff like most in Positano. That means our courtyard and cars are on our flat roof and the house is underneath. After the roof comes the living room and kitchen. Underneath those are our bedrooms. Then underneath *those* is a huge room where Mamma, Papa, and Rocco work and store their guaritore ingredients and tools.

"Your mamma didn't elaborate on what the emergency was, though," Zia Clementina adds.

I fall onto the couch in the living room. Papa and Mamma aren't here, which means I can't tell them about my plan. The nervousness I've felt coiled up inside me all day starts to unwind, but I can't help feeling a little let down, too. Telling Papa is like ripping off a Band-Aid. I just need to get it over with.

"Something to do with Angelo Marini needing help with a large order of gold shiitake mushrooms," she continues. "Right before Christmas Eve. What a hassle!" She pulls her long black hair into a messy bun and stands in front of me, hands on her hips. "Anyway, they're off to Japan tending to that. Rocco will take over their house calls until the situation's sorted. And I'm here to make sure you don't get into any trouble."

I narrow my eyes, remembering Maestra Vita's promise to call home. "What do you know about trouble?"

"I should be asking you that question, Signorina Giada."

Zia Clementina's purple-painted lips turn upward in a grin. "Since you're the one causing so much mischief."

"Did Papa say something?" Panic rises in my voice.

"Your teacher called about twenty minutes after I arrived. Your parents were long gone by then. She told me about your incident in class today."

"What did she say exactly?" I grab one of the blue-and-green-striped throw pillows and hold it against my chest. "Because Maestra Vita isn't exactly my biggest fan."

Zia Clementina sits in the rickety wooden rocking chair near the huge stone hearth opposite me. "She said you showed up late and then caused a disruption. Something about hiding a baby gryphon in your backpack."

"Piccolina was injured. She was sick. I had to help her and then get her back to her mamma. Why is that a bad thing?" I sit up straighter. "It's noble caring for creatures, especially ones that can't care for themselves."

"You don't need to convince me of that," Zia Clementina says. "These instructors want you all to focus your magic on healing people. Ointments that make rashes disappear in minutes and spells that soothe nightmares. Helping more vulnerable creatures doesn't quite fall under that umbrella. Very snobby, if you ask me."

"They're so busy helping humans, they forget about the animals that need protection. Most often from us." I stare at the creases in my palms, wondering what future they foretell. If I'll be happy as a guaritrice or spend my life doing something I don't want to. Would I even get a chance to do what I want? "It's so silly, too. A lot of our ingredients come from animals. Nonna knew that. That's why she took such good care of them. The animals that lived in her garden were well loved and, in return, gave some of the most potent scales, feathers, and toenail clippings in all of the Amalfi Coast. But Papa doesn't ever want to talk about that."

The rocking chair creaks as Zia Clementina stands. "I won't tell your mamma and papa what happened. No need for all their fussing." She holds a hand out to me, smiling. "We can talk more about this later, but for now let's get dinner going. Rocco's readying his rowboat with supplies so you two can get to work as soon as we're finished eating. Maybe we can get some Christmas *and* birthday decorations up after you get back, hmm?"

We walk into the kitchen, my favorite place in the house. It's large, airy, and has big oval doors that open onto a huge balcony covered in flowers. A set of stone stairs winds down from the balcony onto a small backyard of green grass that has a sudden drop-off where there's nothing but the crystal blue Mediterranean Sea.

Zia Clementina opens the fridge, grabs a package wrapped in white paper, and places it on the counter. "Will you help me with the shrimp?" she asks. "It's already washed and deveined. Some salt, pepper, oil, and lemon will do the trick. Maybe some garlic?" She pulls a wooden bowl out from the cabinet and washes arugula in the kitchen sink. "I brought some fresh bread, too. For wiping up the sauce off our plates."

"From Pane Franco?"

"Baked just this morning. I know it's your favorite." She turns on the oven and sets the loaf of bread inside to warm it up.

Outside, the sky grows yellow as the afternoon turns into evening. I open the package of shrimp and empty them into a bowl. The strong scent of seafood wafts through the kitchen, overpowering everything else and filling my lungs. There's nothing I love more than the smell of the ocean. It means home's not far away, and I always want to be here.

I grab the small bowl of salt Mamma keeps near the

stove and sprinkle some over the shrimp. It dissolves quickly, like snowflakes on your tongue.

Zia Clementina dresses the arugula with fresh-squeezed lemon and olive oil. "Giada, can you hand me the Parmesan?" She nods toward the wedge of cheese on the cutting board. "My hands are covered in oil."

I reach for the Parmesan, my arm knocking into the bowl of salt and spilling some over the side. "Madonna mia."

"Make sure to toss the spilled salt over your left shoulder."

My fingers pause just above the salt, when a heavy, burning stench fills my nose. "Uh, Zia?"

BEEP BEEP BEEP BEEP. The smoke alarm blares through the kitchen, a high-pitched noise that rattles in my skull.

"The bread!" Zia Clementina exclaims. She grabs a washcloth off the counter and presses it in my hands. "Open the doors and use this to clear the air."

I hurry to the doors, flinging them open, and snap the washcloth around the kitchen to push the smoke outside. After a moment, the alarm stops beeping. Zia Clementina stands in front of the oven, cradling the charred bread between two oven mitts.

**43**

"It's just a little burnt." I eye the extra–well-done bread. "Maybe we can cut off the burnt parts?"

"That just might work." Zia Clementina smiles and sets the loaf down on the counter near the shrimp. "Remember to use the cheese grater. You don't cut bread with a knife unless you want bad luck."

I pull the grater out of the drawer and carefully grate away the burnt bits of bread. The ash falls away onto the counter in little black bits, revealing a smaller, but not as crispy, loaf.

"Not too bad." Zia Clementina nods in approval as she grates Parmesan over the salad and tops it off with pepper. "Don't forget to clean up."

"Already on it!" I wipe the counter down with the dish towel and push all the charred bits into the sink. "Now what?"

"Did you finish up the shrimp?"

"Of course I—" I clamp my mouth shut as I realize what I've done. The salt! My eyes dart from the shrimp to the bowl of salt, the area around it clean. Oh, no. I wiped the spilled salt away with the burnt bread. I look in the sink and it's too late. It's already dissolving in the water at the bottom of the sink.

"Giada?" Zia Clementina brings a pot of water to boil and grabs the bowl of salt, dumping some in for flavor.

I pull the chef's knife from the block on the counter and start chopping garlic to add to the shrimp. "Just finishing it up now." Panic bounces around my body like a pinball machine. Madonna mia. Tossing spilled salt over your left shoulder is one of the first rules you learn as a strega and one of the most important. It may seem like a silly superstition, but it's an important one. If you don't toss spilled salt over your shoulder, you could get hit with bad luck. And if that's not bad enough, the Streghe del Malocchio—the wicked witches from kids' stories—can actually sniff out a person's bad luck.

The Streghe del Malocchio are old crones who live underground. The malocchio—the jealous, evil eye that can ruin a person's whole life—comes from them. They even steal magic tainted by misfortune. If they find you, they'll whisk you away to their lair, where you'll never see sunlight again. At least that's what the stories say. The knife shakes in my hand, and I put it to the side. *Calm down, Giada. No weird old ladies are going to come for you. They're not real.* I take a deep breath and reach for my cornicello, holding it tight until the tremor in my fingers goes away.

Stars start to poke through the quickly darkening sky. Nighttime always comes faster in the winter, which means work comes earlier for us. It's when Rocco rows out into the sea to beckon the moon and gather her light, plucks basil that's kissed with the gentlest layer of dew, and calls upon Harpies to trade fish for their feathers. He always drags me along to collect these ingredients. Then, if it's not too late, we go on his house calls, where I try to help him heal people but end up sitting in the corner feeling useless and watching for spiders who need help mending their webs.

I grind pepper over the shrimp, black specks covering their gray translucent bodies, and then I add the garlic. Finally, I throw in a splash of olive oil and toss it all together. The bottle is slick in my hands. It slips from between my fingers and crashes to the floor, the dispenser cracking open and drenching the tile.

"What was that?" Zia Clementina turns from the stove to see a puddle of olive oil coating the floor. "Uh-oh." She yanks a towel from the counter and crouches down to clean up the mess. "We can't have bad luck in this house."

Spilled olive oil. Heat creeps up my neck. Another superstition. "Ugh. When it rains, it pours."

"What do you mean?" Zia Clementina arches an eyebrow.

I swallow back the urge to tell her about the salt. If she finds out, she'll make Rocco perform the Malocchio Prayer, a secret spell guaritori learn that gets rid of the nastiest of curses. It's the absolute last resort because it's so complex and uses up a lot of magic. Spilling salt and olive oil don't demand that kind of action. Besides, this was all an accident. I don't have bad luck. My stomach twists. At least I don't think I do.

"Nothing." I shake my head. "It's just been a hard day, is all. I can't seem to catch a break."

"You're a Bellantuono," she reminds me. "You are blessed and important."

My concerns about bad luck are forgotten as today's incident with Maestra Vita comes rushing back. "Legacy. I know, I know. I've gotta live up to my parents' and nonni's and bisnonni's grand reputations among the other guaritori… and not to mention Rocco's. I don't want to think about it."

"Be careful with what you say, Giada." She plates the fettuccine. "Negativity gets you nowhere. It's entirely possible to speak things into existence."

As if on cue, in walks Rocco through the open balcony doors.

# 4

"Giada?" Rocco takes off his boots and tucks them underneath the bench. He strides farther into the kitchen, the familiar scents of sea salt and clean laundry trailing after him. His eyes flicker over to the stove, where Zia Clementina's cooking the shrimp, before landing on me. "A gryphon? In class? Really?"

I cross my arms over my chest. "Yes, a gryphon. Madonna mia. And I don't care what Maestra Vita says about it."

He runs a hand through his thick dark hair. Rocco's just like me. He looks a lot like our parents, with his nearly-black hair, sloping nose, and brown eyes. Except Rocco's the tallest in our family and on the lankier side. I doubt I'll ever grow past five feet, and there's nothing lanky about me, which works out just fine since I love my soft belly and wouldn't want to lose it. Zia Clementina's the same way, and she seems perfectly happy to have never outgrown hers. "A strega needs strength and softness," she always says. "Plump witches get things done."

"Don't be so stubborn. That's what gets you into these messes," he chides.

"Messes?" I look around the kitchen. "I don't see a mess." There are still streaks of oil on the tile, though Rocco hasn't noticed yet.

"Giada, this is serious." Rocco glares, rolling up his sleeves in a way that suggests he means business and that I'm supposed to be afraid. "First it was that ugly tarantula you keep in your garden and now a gryphon?"

"It doesn't have to be serious." I ignore his jab at Tartufo, my lovely, fuzzy tarantula friend who spins magical silk just for me. I also don't bring up Rocco's secret relationship with the gryphons, knowing that'll only set him off. Even though he's being a big old hypocrite. Instead, I twirl around in front of him, arms over my head like a ballerina in a jewelry box.

A smirk creeps over his lips. "Well, Maestra Vita's eyes were bulging out of her head when she was telling me the story. It was *kind of* funny."

I smile at Rocco, patting him on the arm. "See?"

"She was so mad she was clucking like a chicken." Laughter erupts from his belly and bounces around the room. "I wish you could've seen her."

The hilarious image of a Maestra Vita squawking around her classroom in a chicken costume—beak and all—bubbles up in my mind. Soon I'm caught in a fit of giggles of my own.

Rocco takes a deep breath, settling his joy. "In all seriousness, though, you need to focus on becoming an official guaritrice. Maestra Vita's very concerned. When Papa finds out, he's—"

"Papa's *not* finding out." The smile on my face is replaced with a scowl.

Zia Clementina clears her throat. "Dinner's almost ready."

Rocco shakes his head. He grabs three plates and bowls from one of the cabinets and walks into the dining room without saying another word.

"He's gonna tell on me. Typical Rocco." The shrimp sizzle in the pan as they turn an opaque pink.

"I'll talk to him later," Zia Clementina promises. "Here." She rips off a chunk of the now less burnt bread and swirls it in the olive oil she mixed with rosemary and garlic. "Have some bread. Cures all."

The bread is soft and chewy and smells like the wood-fired oven it was baked in. A sharp hint of garlic comes right behind. My favorite. I could eat a whole jar of peeled garlic. The earthy herb and olive flavors linger on my tongue. Normally we save the bread for the end of dinner to clean up the extra sauce. It's called scarpetta, and it's the best part of the meal. But Zia Clementina likes olive oil with her bread, and so do I, even if it's not the norm. For a minute I feel guilty about eating so much bread, but I can't resist. Zia Clementina doesn't seem too worried about it, so I push the thought out of my head.

"Good, isn't it?" Zia Clementina tears a bit off for herself. "I'm telling you, there's nothing a hunk of fresh-baked bread and a little garlic can't fix. Food's as magical as anything else." She hands me some silverware and napkins. "Now, go help your brother set the table. And no more trouble."

I roll my eyes. "Fine, but only for you."

"I appreciate it," Zia Clementina says in a singsong voice. "Go head into the dining room. I'll be right behind you with the food."

Rocco's wiping crumbs off the table and setting the plates and bowls. He doesn't look up at me when I start placing the silverware and napkins.

"Madonna mia, Rocco. Papa doesn't need to know. It's not that big of a deal. You were laughing just a minute ago," I protest, tucking the last napkin underneath its plate and settling into my chair. "Don't give me the silent treatment."

"You didn't have to bring the gryphon with you to class." He sits down across from me, pressing his hand to his temple.

I idly spin my fork on its tines. "I couldn't leave Piccolina to fend for herself. She needed to be reunited with her mamma."

Zia Clementina comes in, balancing a hefty plate of fettuccine tossed with the shrimp and some extra olive oil in one hand and the salad in the other. "Just need to go back for the bread and water!" She disappears into the kitchen, humming an upbeat tune.

Ever since Rocco took the oath, he's become so much more like Papa. So serious about his profession. But I understand why he's devoted to fixing people. Rocco took his oath the Christmas before the pandemic hit. In the beginning, Italy was one of the most affected countries. So many people got sick. So many people died. Rocco, Papa, Mamma, and all the other guaritori worked around the clock on tonics and salves and spells to keep patients strong enough to fight the illness. But it wasn't easy. Ingredients ran out. Guaritori exhausted themselves. Guaritori don't cure, they strengthen. And there was only so much strengthening that could be done. As much as Rocco annoys me, I can't imagine graduating from training and walking right into all of that.

"Doing what makes me happy and using my magic to take care of creatures is the right thing. What's wrong with that? It's the same as you helping people, but with mermaids and three-headed dogs."

Rocco looks up at me but doesn't respond.

Zia Clementina returns and pours water into our glasses. She places the bread on the table and sits down next to me. "Start eating before it gets cold."

We fill our plates in silence, the scraping of forks and spoons echoing.

Zia Clementina clears her throat. "So, Giada. Your birthday's only a week away. The lucky thirteen. *Plus*, the guaritore oath ceremony is a week later. It's a big year for you! What do you want to do to celebrate? The regular dinner and cake? I should make fresh cannoli."

"I don't know." I hesitate, fidgeting with my napkin. The speech I had rehearsed for my talk with Papa ricochets off every nerve in my brain. If I don't tell him as soon as he gets back, it'll be too late to back out of the ceremony. "Nothing, probably. I don't want to puke it up because I'm anxious."

"What's there to be anxious about?" Rocco asks. "You're a Bellantuono. You'll ace the ceremony." He points his fork in my direction, lips twitching into a smile. "*If* you play by the rules from here on out."

"Well, what if I don't want to?" I tear off a hunk of bread and dip it in olive oil. "What if I just didn't do it?"

His eyes widen. "Why wouldn't you?"

I look down at my plate, my heart pounding in my chest like a caged lion. Now's the time to say something, but

I prepared for Papa's disappointment. Not Rocco's. "For one, I don't want to do the apprenticeship."

Rocco cuts the tail off a shrimp. "You'll learn so much training with another guaritore family," he states through a mouthful of food. "I wish I had the experience."

Apprenticeships are a new tradition that began after the pandemic. Guaritore families used to share nothing with each other unless a family merged in marriage. Like a closely guarded marinara recipe that's been passed down through the ages, guaritori didn't want to give away their methods. It was a point of pride, but pretty selfish, if you ask me. Most of the families realized this wasn't a good idea during the pandemic. It was dangerous refusing to share knowledge that could help save lives. So, to spread the methods that were once kept secret, it was decided that new guaritori would have an apprenticeship with another family and learn some of their tricks. Which is all nice and good, but I still don't want to do it.

I take a sip of water to push down the lump in my throat and ask, "What if I don't want to do any of it?" Madonna mia. All the nerve I built up to tell Papa is seeping out. I have to spill the beans about my plan to someone tonight or I'll never do it. Zia Clementina will be proud of me no matter what I want to do, but unfortunately, I'm not so sure about Rocco.

Zia Clementina places her fork down next to her plate and sighs. From the corner of my eye I see her open her mouth to say something, but Rocco's too quick.

"Not do any of it," he repeats. "What are you talking about?"

There's never going to be a better time than this. It's now or never. "First of all, I don't want to do the apprenticeship because it won't focus on what I want to do with my magic." I hold up two fingers to emphasize my point. "Second of all, I don't know if I want to take the oath and become an official healer. Third of all, I don't feel a connection to Apollo like you and the rest of the guaritori do. I love Diana more. She protects animals."

The last point is hard to say aloud. But I've been practicing it for a long time. Streghe all have similar threads of magic sewn into their bones, but there are those who have strengths in particular kinds of magic.

Rocco launches into a tirade. "The alchemists don't abandon Vulcan. They respect him as the god of blacksmithing and alchemy. Oracles would never abandon Minerva and refuse her wisdom. For you to disrespect

Apollo, our god of medicine, the averter of the evil eye, everyone's protector from malocchio…"

I purse my lips. I know he's waiting for me to take it back, to say I didn't mean it. But I won't. "I said what I meant and meant what I said. You can stop looking at me like that."

Rocco's mouth hangs open. "You can't just not take the oath."

"Why not?" I ask. "Zia Clementina didn't take the oath. She's an oracle, and you just said oracles wouldn't abandon Minerva. Wouldn't I actually be abandoning Diana since I feel connected to her and not Apollo?"

Zia Clementina moves to speak, but is cut off once again.

"This is different." Rocco's cheeks flush pink. He glances from Zia Clementina to me. "You're my sister. We're supposed to be in this together."

"Just because it's the family business doesn't mean it's my dream."

Rocco presses his forefinger and thumb into his eyelids. His face is now pomodoro red. His jaw twitches. A pit opens up in my stomach. He looks just like Papa. "It's an honor to be blessed by Apollo and to take on this responsibility. You can't just choose to identify with a different god because you feel like it." He drums his fingers on the table as he continues, "You have to help *people*, Giada. There's only so much magic to go around, and you can't waste it on animals. Some say choosing to follow another god is bad luck even the Malocchio Prayer can't fix."

"Zia Clementina doesn't have bad luck."

"Hey now," Zia Clementina shouts, waving her arms as she tries to get our attention. "Don't talk about Zia Clementina like she's not here. And no more arguing at the table, please."

Rocco's head droops a little and he eyes our zia, murmuring, "It goes against the rules, Giada."

"All these rules!" I toss my hands in the air. "Maybe I don't care about the rules!" I consider calling Rocco out on his relationship with the gryphons. How he's bending the rules to cultivate a bond in order to get the best of their feathers for the secret tonic he's working on. The one he's too afraid to tell Papa about. But I bite my tongue. He's only told me about it, and if I brought it up now, in front of Zia Clementina, this fight would ramp all the way up to level 100.

"Think of the legacy you'd be abandoning. The Bellantuonos come from a long line of important guaritori. You must follow."

"I. Don't. Care." I throw my napkin onto my barely eaten dinner, even though fettuccine is my favorite, my face and neck hot with anger.

"I don't want you coming with me tonight." Rocco braces his hands against the table, his own face as red as mine feels. "You're an embarrassment to our family, Giada."

"Rocco!" Zia Clementina shouts. "Basta!"

But the damage is done. My vision blurs with tears. It's too late for him to take back what he said. I push away from the table and hurry out of the dining room, race down the stairs to my bedroom, slam the door shut behind me. Tears fall fast, leaving salty trails in their wake. I wipe them away with my sleeve and curl up on my bed with a fluffy green blanket.

"Ridiculous Rocco," I mutter into my pillow. Even he isn't the perfect guaritore. If Papa knew about what he was up to with his tonic, he'd say it's too ambitious or experimental. Rocco's creating a tonic to help with depression. He sought out the pride of gryphons who live here for their rare feathers and claw clippings. These ingredients, willingly given, create light and protection. And they're usually hard to come by because guaritori don't often work with animals. But Rocco's forging a relationship with them. I caught him sneaking off after a house call one night. If he gets it right, when a person drinks the tonic, their inner light will be restored. It would be the first of its kind. But that doesn't mean Papa would be happy with him toeing the line of nontraditional.

"Giada?" Zia Clementina knocks, her voice soft on the other side of the door. "Can I come in?"

"No." I jump from the bed and turn off my light. "I'm going to sleep."

"Are you sure? We can talk."

"I'll be fine."

Silence. Finally, Zia Clementina sighs. "All right. I'm here if you need me."

I hear her walk down the hallway as I climb back into bed. My room is dark, and with the window wide open, letting the night air in, it feels even darker. Wind whispers through the lemon trees in our narrow backyard, rustling the leaves. I wrap the blanket tighter around my body and lie at the edge of my bed, staring up at the moon. She's partially hidden by storm clouds, and her shine isn't as bright as it usually is. Rocco will still gather as much of her light as he can. He always does.

I roll onto my side. Maybe I *do* have bad luck. Maybe I've had it all my life. With a brother as annoying as Rocco, it's possible. "I wish he'd just disappear."

It's not a nice thing to say. But if Rocco wasn't around, it'd be easier for me to do what I want. I wouldn't always be compared to him. I could be my own person.

I watch through the window as Rocco trudges down the balcony steps, lantern held high. He ducks under the pergola with its overgrown bougainvillea, slips between the lemon and silk floss trees. I always go with him to moon beckon. Hurt creeps into my heart, and I cross my arms over my chest to keep it from spreading.

The wind blows through my window again, this time strong enough to whip up my pink rose curtains.

I scurry out of bed and shut it. Rocco's at the cliff's edge and is making his way down the stairs to the grotto where our family keeps the rowboat.

Only one week left until my thirteenth birthday, and then I'll have to make a choice before the ceremony. One that'll either disappoint my family or myself. I lean against the cool windowsill, trying to find the moon amid the clouds, but she's completely gone now. A storm's picking up.

I turn to climb back into bed, but there's a flicker out there in the dark. I squint into the night, trying to make out the shape. The clouds pass just enough for the moon's light to cast a soft glow over the backyard.

The hairs on my neck stand.

Looking up at me from underneath the pergola is a black cat. Yet another superstition.

The salt. The olive oil. And now a black cat. It can't be a coincidence. Can it?

A headache forms at the back of my head as I try to piece together what it could all mean. That's the thing about luck—it's so confusing that thinking too hard about it will make you dizzy.

I leap into bed and jam my eyes shut.

"You're fine. You're safe," I whisper to the darkness of my bedroom. "The Streghe del Malocchio won't come get you. Not for small things like salt and oil." Worry edges its way into my thoughts, but I shake my head until it disappears. "That's all make-believe anyway."

Lightning cracks open the sky, and rain lashes against my window. But it's the faint howling that turns my blood cold. A long, mournful howl that might belong to the wind racing between the trees. Or to a black cat, patiently waiting to deliver more bad luck.

# 5

Even though it was mean to wish for Rocco to disappear, I was annoyed it didn't come true when he started banging on my door to wake me up bright and early this morning. He made sure my uniform was pressed, my hair was braided, and I wasn't late, going as far as to bike with me to class. And the worst part was that Maestra Vita was so pleased to see Rocco that she insisted he stick around to answer questions before we started our lesson. Everyone but me was excited to have the great Rocco Bellantuono as a special guest.

My eyes got sore from how much I rolled them.

"I know you don't like talking about Rocco, but it was pretty cool having him talk to our class today," Alessia exclaims as we walk our bikes down the hill back into town after school. "I can't believe that he single-handedly freed a convent of nuns from a contagious case of night terrors with nothing but a single fig bathed in moonlight."

I roll my eyes. Again. At this rate I'll have to take some Riparazione Oculare drops from Mamma and Papa's storeroom. "Yeah, well, the nuns wouldn't have gotten night terrors if he had fortified their convent from the malocchio to begin with."

"I hope he comes back to teach a lesson."

"Oh, I'm sure he'd love that."

Alessia frowns and pushes a hair behind her ear. "Ugh. I'm sorry. I'll stop talking about it."

"It's fine." I give her a smile. "I know you're excited about all of this. And you should be! I'm just so tired of hearing about Rocco."

We walk our bikes down the narrow road that curves into Positano. Alessia and I live downhill from school, the heart of the city in between the Torre di Apollo and our homes. We pass all the beautiful sandstone houses peeking out of the cliff side like freckles on a great big mountain. Trees and flowers crawl along beside them, and there's always a view of the sea. Christmas decorations are already up, too. Everything's decorated in glittering lights and big silver bows. Shop owners wave at us. A few kids stare and whisper to one another.

We turn a corner, and a streak of black darts in front of us. Right in front of Salvatore's Tailoring.

"What was that?" Alessia asks.

"Nothing. A shadow. Probably." My stomach drops. That black cat from last night sits on the other side of the street, his eyes a bright green, his black whiskers twitching.

She continues her yakking about how awesome my brother is.

I squint at the cat. Everyone, especially extra superstitious people like Zia Clementina, swears that black cats aren't to be messed around with. But he's a cute little fella. Too cute to be a real bad omen. He yawns, big eyes squeezed tight, and my heart swells. The urge to cross the street and give him endless pets and cuddles buzzes against my bones in the same way my magic does. He could need my help. Or, at the very least, he could need a warm bed and a friend. But Alessia would likely yell at me if I went over to see what was up with him. She's just

**66**

like my zia and has so many superstitions you'd think she was born a little old strega, always worrying about this and that.

Then I remember how spooky the cat was last night. Like he was watching me in the dark.

"Let's hurry up." I grip the handles of my bike tighter and quicken my pace down the street.

His eyes trail us, and then he hops down.

"Don't follow us," I grumble under my breath.

"What was that?" Alessia asks.

"Nothing."

"Talking to yourself again?" She nudges me with her elbow, giggling. "Remember that one sleepover we had with Isabella and Francesca? Before Isabella became all… ugh. You woke us up mumbling in your sleep about dancing centaurs."

"I'll have you know, sleep talking is perfectly normal, thank you very much."

"Sure, sure. But the sleep singing you did the last time you slept over at my house?" Alessia smirked. "I don't know about that…"

The cat trots along the other side of the street from us,

hopping up onto the stairs and stealthily dodging potted plants.

I keep stealing glances at him as I pass by the ancient knobby-looking walnut tree that sits in the middle of the square. The one as a kid I always thought was watching us. Maybe the cat is headed there. Hopefully.

The wind kicks up. Purple clouds swirl over the sea, and lightning strikes the water like cracks in a porcelain vase.

"Hmm…might rain," I say. Cats hate rain. Maybe he'll go hide.

"Oh, no!" Alessia twists her backpack around to the front of her body and puts a protective arm over it. "I've got all my study guides in here. And my practitioner's notebook! They can't get wet."

I turn away from the cat, but that doesn't stop him from stalking after me as if I were a tasty mouse he couldn't wait to gobble.

*Get a grip, Giada.* But my heart hurls itself against my ribs as memories of spilling the salt and olive oil replay in my head on a loop.

Thunder grumbles close by. People hurry off the street looking for cover.

The cat still follows me. He should be running for a

warm, dry place like everybody else. But he keeps pace with us, unbothered.

Alessia glances over at him, an eyebrow raised. "Giada, look at that big black cat." She touches her cornicello, shaking her head. "Is he watching us?"

Without thinking, I yank Alessia into the nearest shop, both of us dropping our bikes on the street. "Hey!" Alessia squeaks, freeing herself from my hand and giving me a look. "Why'd you do that?"

"It's gonna get bad out there before we can get home. May as well ride out the storm here." I look around, not realizing I dragged us into a souvenir shop meant for tourists. "Ooh, magnets!" I point to a display with photos of Positano, the Torre di Apollo, and even a few of the lucciole, the pretty fireflies that zip through our city spreading their magic when the sun goes down. "I love magnets."

Alessia arches an eyebrow, her arms crossed. "You're acting weirder than normal. Like you're hiding something."

"Me? Hide something?" I laugh, my eyes drifting toward the shop's window. The black cat lingers outside, grooming his whiskers. "Couldn't even hide that gryphon for very long."

"At least this store connects to the café next door. Let's

go in there," she suggests. "Unless you really want magnets of the city you live in."

We walk into the café. Rain patters against the roof and dribbles down the window in heavy streams, nearly drowning out the pop music playing. Alessia gets an affogato, a scoop of vanilla gelato with a shot of espresso poured over the top.

"Can I please have a scoop of hazelnut gelato with whipped cream on top?"

The man serving us looks me up and down. "Are you sure you want whipped cream, too?"

"Yeah, that's why I asked for it." I put my hands on my hips and stand straighter. This is why I like animals better than people. They don't stare at you like you're doing something wrong when you're just ordering the food you want.

He says nothing and gives me my gelato with whipped cream. I eat a big spoonful, and sigh, "Yummmm. So good. I could eat a hundred of them. Maybe I will. 'Cause I can eat whatever I want."

He scurries away.

We sit down at one of the pink-and-purple polka-dot tables in the corner of the café. Alessia pulls a huge binder from her backpack and flips it open to a pocket holding a thick stack of flash cards. Next, she grabs her small camel leather practitioner's notebook from the front pocket and places it carefully to the side. I never even bothered starting my own practitioner's notebook, much to Rocco's annoyance. He always says I need to be more like Alessia and take things seriously. Her notebook is so neat, so precise. Just what a guaritrice *should* have. But her process doesn't work for me. And I do take notes, just not on guaritore magic. Her notebook is much more organized than my vet's log, which largely consists of hastily scribbled down spells, smears of dirt and waterlogged pages from using it in the field, and doodles of creatures. But it suits me just fine.

Once she's gotten her study materials in order, Alessia asks, "What's up with you?"

"Nothing."

Alessia's eyes dart up to me, and she gasps, "Madonna mia. Did you tell your family about your plan?"

"My parents went to help your zio with those mushrooms, so I couldn't tell them yet. But I told Rocco."

"How'd it go?" she asks before slurping down another spoonful of her affogato.

"Well…" I trail off.

"I'm proud of you for telling him." Alessia pats my hand. "Carrying secrets around is bad for your health."

"Thanks."

"Rocco will come around. And your parents will, too, once you tell them."

I take a bite of my gelato. "I don't want to talk about it anymore."

"Want to test me instead?" Alessia flutters her lashes and passes me her flash cards. "Oh, don't make that face."

"You know all of it already! You're gonna ace it."

She sighs. "I know you're not excited, but the oath ceremony's gonna be so cool. My nonna even made me, like, a guaritore advent calendar. There's a gift for every day leading up to Christmas Eve. A bird popped out of it this morning. It's just the best."

Because the Malocchio Prayer is strongest on Christmas Eve, that's when the oath ceremony is held, regardless of when you turn thirteen during the year. We take the oath and then learn the prayer, in secret, and perform it for good luck during our apprenticeship. Then, we start our apprenticeships in January.

"You'll finally get to take the oath. After almost a whole

year." I grin at her. "Maybe you'll stop being a ball of nerves."

Alessia turned thirteen last February and had to keep going to Maestra Vita's class. Waiting has made her a little intense. She thinks I'm lucky since my birthday is only a week before Christmas Eve.

I dip my spoon in the whipped cream, asking, "Is your mom still crying over you leaving for your apprenticeship?"

"I think she's gotten used to the idea. But now she's sewing cloves of garlic into my clothes for extra protection, which is totally embarrassing. I don't want to smell funky when I'm meeting my host family."

"You're her first kid going away." I shrug. "Maybe she'll get over it and won't be so nervous when Michele turns thirteen."

"Maybe," she says. "Now test me. Just one question!"

"Oh, fine. Just the one, though." I shuffle through her flash cards, picking one from the middle at random. On the front, the word POINTING is written in Alessia's big loopy cursive. On the back is a lengthy definition. "Tell me all about pointing."

Alessia blinks once, twice, then hops in her seat, ready

with the answer. "When treating a patient, you must never describe their disease or illness by pointing at your own body. Like if the patient has a headache or sore throat, you shouldn't point to your head or throat because then you may get sick. Actions like that have power, and magic is strongest in a guaritore's hands." Her eyes shine with excitement as she rambles off the perfect response. She drinks some of her affogato before continuing. "And if you accidentally do this, be sure to make a cross over the places you pointed to. Doing that will get rid of the evil that could infect your body. Making the sign of the cross also blesses and helps with healing."

"See? You know this stuff." I toss her flash cards onto her binder with a grin. "There's such a thing as too much studying, you know."

"I bought a new potion book—*Chicken Soup and 101 Other Potions for the Soul*—from that strega merchant who works out of the trinket shop near Fornillo Beach. I can't wait to actually create my own potions and spells and not just practice in Maestra Vita's classroom." She stirs her spoon through her drink, the ice cream already melted. "Do you think maybe Rocco would show me a few techniques early?"

"Your first time healing is supposed to be with your family before you're sent away to another city for your apprenticeship. That's the tradition," I remind her. The excitement drops from her face. "I'm sorry, that came out weird. What I meant was that Rocco takes it all so seriously that he wouldn't want you to miss out on the tradition."

Alessia smiles. "Yeah, you're right. It's just so hard being patient. I want to do it all *right now*. The way Maestra Vita and the other teachers talk about it, I am so excited to make people feel better. There's probably nothing like experiencing it."

*Why can't I be as excited as she is about it all?* I eat a bite of hazelnut gelato and let the flavors melt on my tongue, hoping it might change how I feel. "Helping people is great, but it's tough, too. You're out every night gathering ingredients that'll go bad after only a few hours and are dangerous to get. Then you have to hike up and down the city making house calls. Some are easy requests for things you have on hand or can be healed with a simple spell, like scraped knees or bad bruises. But other visits take hours. And people can be so grumpy."

"Maestra Vita has said over and over that it's hard work."

"It's more than that," I counter. "Last week Rocco dragged

me to a farmhouse on top of a cliff. Inside was an old man that was hit so hard with the malocchio he had *two* evil spirits sitting on his chest at night, giving him sleep paralysis. We were there until dawn, and it was so frustrating. I'm not good at keeping calm around people."

"It's not fair that your mamma and papa let you go with Rocco before taking your oath." Alessia points her spoon at me. "*That's* not tradition."

"It isn't fair," I agree. "I wish I could trade places with you since you'd actually love it. But I'm glad they let me go with Rocco, otherwise I wouldn't know what I'm getting myself into. Now I know for sure I don't want to become a healer. Well, at least not that kind of healer."

Her expression softens. "You're gonna be great no matter what. And it'll work out with your parents when you tell them. Maybe by the time they get back from their trip, Rocco will have gotten used to the idea and will have your back."

"Yeah, we'll see about that. You know how he is." I think about Rocco calling me an embarrassment and bury it down with another bite of my dessert. "They'll come around. Maybe. Or they'll deal. The guaritori have Rocco, and it's not like I was going to be that great with helping people anyway."

"When it all works out with your family—because it will—what's part two of the plan? Traveling across the globe to heal all sorts of creatures?" Alessia wiggles her eyebrows, making me laugh.

I look down at my empty gelato dish, a smile inching over my face. "I've been experimenting with potions that use lavender and mermaid scales and seawater and the west wind. I want to set up my own shop. Or maybe a sanctuary where injured creatures can be healed and come to rest. I'll use all the spells and potions to help them."

Alessia leans back in her chair, tilting her head to the side as she looks at me. "If there's anyone who can do all of that, it's you."

Her encouragement wraps around my heart and squeezes tight. It almost makes up for Rocco's reaction last night. "Thank you," I murmur, my face hot.

"Either that or you're going underground to become a Strega del Malocchio or something," she teases.

Even though I'm still a little worried after the mishaps last night, the thought of becoming an evil old lady who

77

spends her days souring cow's milk and giving teenagers acne makes me snort. "If you misbehave, I'll turn your hair into a bird's nest and suck the marrow from your bones," I whisper in a croaky old crone's voice, pointing a crooked finger at Alessia.

She giggles, swatting my hand away. "Are you going to replace my ears with tomatoes, too?"

"Only if you don't brush your teeth before bed." While our superstitions may hold truth, I'm old enough now to know the stories parents would tell us about a coven of witches whose magic comes from the evil eye were just that. Stories. Fairy tales used to scare kids into behaving.

The storm starts to let up a little, but dark clouds still hang in the sky. We throw away our paper cups before heading back out onto the drizzly cool street. The cat's nowhere to be found, thankfully. The rain must've driven him away. We jump through puddles, splashing in the mud, and my worries get smaller with every giggle.

Black cats are just animals. And maybe he knew I was the right kind of helper. That if he was sick or hurt, I was the person to come to. Regret nags at me for not going to him and seeing if he was all right.

First order of business when I open my own guaritore animal clinic: fix what everyone thinks of black cats.

We grab our bikes and ride down a winding road to the quieter, less frequented part of the city where the three strega families who take care of the Amalfi Coast have lived for centuries. There are others, of course, but our families are the biggest in the area.

The Marinis and Bellantuonos are the guaritori. Alessia's family is renowned like ours, but in a different way. While we're known for our innovation in the field, they're known for being the best at healing physical things like broken bones and nasty wounds. Even before guaritori were comfortable sharing some of their secrets, the Marinis and Bellantuonos were always happy to trade ingredients and help each other out with potions and spell work. It's why my parents were so quick to travel all the way to Japan to help out Alessia's zio.

The third family, the Ferraros, are alchemists. It's not unusual to hear loud explosions or see different-colored plumes of smoke coming from their house. They usually keep to themselves but lend us a hand with our more complex elixirs.

We stop in front of Alessia's house and, even several feet

from the front door, the warm scent of something yummy wafts through the air. My stomach grumbles. Alessia claps her hands together. "Mamma and Michele are making chicken soup and bread. My favorite. Do you want to stay and eat with us? Michele's been asking about the baby gryphon ever since I told him about what happened in class." She put a hand to her mouth, snorting.

I shake my head. "I would, but Rocco's keeping a close eye on me until Mamma and Papa get home. But say hi to your parents and brother for me, yeah?"

Alessia waves goodbye, then hurries inside to get out of the weather.

I get on my bike and speed home. The wind whips against my face and kicks up the musky, salty scents of sea and sand. I love winter storms. They're the best. So cozy after days of endless sweating and sun so bright it leaves spots in your vision. Fresh rainwater's also one of the most important ingredients in some of my potions since it inspires growth and renewal. Not that I'd ever raise my hand to answer one of Maestra Vita's questions.

My house comes into view, and I hop off my bike, parking it by the front gate. I check on the pails I keep hidden in the garden Nonna helped me plant a few years ago.

It's not nearly as large or lush as hers was, but with time it could be.

When I was a little girl, before I began my guaritore homeschooling, I'd spend most of my time with my nonna. Papa and Mamma were busy with work and with training Rocco, so I'd walk down the street to her tiny bright blue house with the yellow-tiled courtyard and wisteria vines creeping up the walls, and we'd play in her garden. She had all sorts of plants. Normal ones like olive trees and tomato vines, but also magical and sometimes dangerous plants like belladonna and giant hogweed.

Nonna taught me to love animals. Tucked away between geranium bushes and in the limbs of lemon trees lived creatures like gold-bellied snakes and butterflies the size of my hand that could change the winds with a flutter of their wings. It's like they knew my nonna would keep them safe.

She was always tending to her plants and the creatures who called her garden home, caring for them with so much love. In exchange they blessed her with treasures like ruby-red tomatoes or gold snakeskin. When guaritori ran out of ingredients, my nonna was the one they'd come to.

But even though Papa loved his mamma, he thought all her work was just a hobby. That she should have spent more time fixing people and less time in her garden. It was something they argued about every now and then. Especially as I got older and started homeschooling. Papa wanted to make it clear that what Nonna did was nice but not a priority over healing people.

I tap one of my silver pails and watch the rainwater vibrate. All three pails are nearly halfway full. Not too bad. Hopefully there's more rain to come, but I'll have to use it quick. Three days only. After three days it loses its power and has to be tossed out.

"Tartufo? You home?" I squint into the dark knot where he built his home. Tartufo's nearly as old as my garden. One day when weeding my patch of wolfsbane, I felt a little tickle on my shoulder. He'd heard me whistling and decided to move right in. Ever since, he's been my very best helper, spinning the silk I use in all of my weaving and binding spells. Spider silk is extra strong and is good for holding together ingredients that aren't as sticky, like moonlight or sea fog. It's the same spider silk I use to create Rocco's fishing nets—the best fishing nets on the

Amalfi Coast. Tartufo's kept full and happy in exchange for his work, getting plenty of beetles in return.

Eight black eyes stare back at me, each blinking in a pattern that means ciao. Just because I'm good with creatures doesn't mean I can talk to them like I would a person, but it's easier for me to communicate with creatures. It takes a bit of my magic but not enough to really tire me out. Not all streghe can talk to animals and it's one thing I do better than Rocco. He doesn't understand Tartufo or the other creatures that find their way to me.

"Ciao, Tartufo. Lovely to see you today," I greet before tossing him a grasshopper from the pocket of my bag.

He happily munches on its crunchy legs, and I wipe my hands on my skirt, leaving dirty streaks behind.

The sun's starting to set behind the storm-colored sea. Dusk's my favorite time of the day. Lucciole float out from the trees and fly around my garden, their lights winking in the ever-growing dark. Some streghe say the fireflies are the ghosts of ancestors, which would make sense since they only come out to shine at night. They're also drawn to magic. It's like a bath for them, warm and inviting. Rocco and I are always followed by them when we moon beckon.

I like having them around. Their glow brings peace and helps streghe better focus their magic.

I watch them gather for a few more minutes before turning toward the front door.

I jump. Sitting on the blue and orange tiles of our small courtyard, almost camouflaged by my dark green front door, is the black cat. He stares at me with his bright green eyes, unblinking, and concern blossoms in my belly.

"Hey," I coo before clicking my tongue to try and coax him over. "Do you want some help?"

The cat's ears twitch, but he stays put. Wet but completely unbothered as he grooms his long whiskers.

"You hurt?" I ask.

When he doesn't move, panic twists its way through my body like a weed, choking out my previous concern. I think about him lurking in the night and following me and Alessia through town. He showed up right after the salt and olive oil incidents. Maybe I can't fix what people think of black cats. Maybe they are just another sign of bad luck.

"You need something?"

Nothing.

I take a deep breath, the panic now all-consuming. He

clearly doesn't want my help. Snapping, I shout, "Okay. Then leave me alone!" I flail my arms in front of me and charge at the cat. "Shoo!"

He trots away from my front door and hides underneath a nearby mimosa tree, his back to the sea.

"Go back to wherever you came from! Shoo!"

He stretches out underneath the tree's bright yellow blooms. He's not going anywhere. At least for the time being. The panic that's taken hold of me tightens. Without moving my eyes off him, I back up the stairs and hurry through the front door, locking it behind me. I lean against the door, breathing hard.

Maybe he just likes me. Most animals do.

Or he could be an omen. A sign that I do have bad luck and it's about to get worse.

I squeeze my cornicello in my fist. Whatever he is, I'll need to come up with a way to get rid of him. Fast.

**6**

"Pass the salad, Giada," Rocco says. I look away from him and stab a tomato.

"Will you please pass the salad to your brother?" Zia Clementina asks.

"Can an *embarrassment* even pass the salad?" I taunt with my mouth full. "Are we capable?"

"Giada." Zia Clementina gives me the look adults always give you when you're pushing against the limit of their patience. "Let's have a nice dinner."

"I'm not sure if I can." I poke at a cucumber. "What with being an embarrassment and all."

"I didn't mean that."

"Just because I'm not the *Amazing Rocco Bellantuono* doesn't mean I'm any less."

Rocco reaches across the table for the bowl of salad and plates a second helping. "You're being dramatic."

"So now I'm an embarrassment *and* dramatic?" I toss my hands in the air, voice so high I'm practically squeaking. "You always say things like that. I'm too dramatic, too loud, too bossy. I'm always doing too much of something."

"Basta! That's enough from both of you." Zia Clementina looks between us. "Let's have a pleasant conversation."

"An embarrassment will never be pleasant. Ever."

"Eat your salad, Giada."

The clock on the wall ticks out the seconds. The little white Christmas lights Zia Clementina hung blink on and off. Thunder echoes outside. Tension rises in the room like heat on an asphalt road. Rocco and I always bicker, but it's never been like this. I take a sip of my water and look at him. His jaw is tight, his bushy eyebrows knit together.

"Where's your cornicello?" I ask, eyeing the space where the gold horn should be hanging around his neck.

"Chain broke. I need to get a new one," he says without looking up.

"It's dangerous using magic without your cornicello," I whisper. I touch mine as I say it. My nonna gave me mine when I was born, and I don't think I've ever taken it off.

He shrugs. "I went out without it before and was fine. I know what I'm doing."

"But that's because I had mine. I'm always with you."

Zia Clementina takes a deep breath. "I went to the market today, which is where I picked up the sea bass we had, and I saw the funniest little dog outside of the butcher's chomping on a huge bone. It was twice his size!"

Rocco and I both force laughter and go back to finishing our meal in silence. As soon as he's done, he stands and starts clearing plates.

"Leaving early again?" Zia Clementina asks.

"There's a lot to be done until the Marinis can purchase another six pounds of mushrooms," Rocco mentions, carrying dishes toward the kitchen. "Papa says it'll be another few days at the minimum."

"But they'll be back for your birthday." Zia Clementina looks at me before getting up to help Rocco clear the rest of the table. "That's what they said earlier today."

"I don't mind. Really," I protest. At least I have more time to figure out how I'm gonna tell them about my plan. After Rocco's reaction, the more time the better.

I follow Zia Clementina into the kitchen with my plate and the platter of leftover sea bass. Rocco's already washing dishes.

"Looks like it's going to rain harder tonight than it did yesterday," Zia Clementina remarks. It's already past sunset, but a flash of lightning illuminates the storm ahead. She eyes the fat purple clouds warily. "Can you beckon the moon in this weather?"

"It'll clear up some. I need moonlight to ward off a little girl's nightmares." Rocco's always too stubborn to listen to reason. Of course he's gonna go out on the sea in all this rain and lightning.

My belly knots with anxiety. "She can have nightmares for one more night. It's dangerous out there."

He looks at me, his eyes soft. "I've been out in worse. I can handle it."

The wind picks up, practically shrieking as it slams into our house. Another bolt of lightning strikes the sea and breaks the sky in two.

"I'll stay close to the shore until it calms down." Rocco

wipes his soapy hands with a dish towel and immediately starts lacing up his boots and tossing on a black coat. He grabs his lantern off its hook and lights it. "See you later. Try not to get into any trouble while I'm gone, Giada."

Madonna mia. He's never not going to see me as his annoying little sister. He'll never respect me.

The door flies open, and Rocco struggles to close it behind him. Zia Clementina and I watch from the window as he fights against the wind, the candle in his lantern already snuffed out.

That same anxiety swirls up once more, but I do my best to tamp it down. Rocco's gonna be fine. Like always. If anything, this'll just make him look like even more of a hero in everybody's eyes. It's probably why he's doing it—to get one step closer to having his portrait hanging in the Torre di Apollo as one of the best guaritori to ever live. Typical Rocco.

*You're an embarrassment to our family.* I wrap up the leftovers and slam the refrigerator door shut. He'd never be an embarrassment. He's perfect.

"Want to help me tidy up a bit before bed?" Zia Clementina asks. She heads into the laundry room and returns with a basket of clean sheets. "I'm glad I got the washing

done and these off the line before it started storming."
She takes the basket into the dining room and starts folding the sheets on the table. "I'll handle this if you can take
care of the living room."

I grab the hand broom and dustpan from the closet
before shuffling into the living room. Throwing open the
window, I pull a bit of the magic from way down in my
belly. It's a lot like singing. You gotta breathe deep from
your diaphragm to wake up the power. That familiar tingle
vibrates through my bones, spreading out into my fingertips and toes. No matter how much of our magic we're
using, conjuring it up is always the same.

"Vieni qui! Come here, little ones," I shout out the window as thunder rumbles. Magic tickles the back of my
throat, just as it had when healing the mamma gryphon.
"I need your help."

A big purple lizard scurries over the ledge, down the
wall, and up onto the coffee table. She's followed by a pair
of bright white doves flying out of the storm and alight-
ing on one of the huge wooden bookcases. A mouse with
red eyes scurries out from under the couch. The four of
them stare up at me, and I grin. It was after I first saw *Snow*

*White* that I thought about asking my animal friends to help me with chores.

"Thank you for coming. Could you please help me clean up?" I pull a brown paper bag out of my backpack. "There are blackberries in it for you."

They blink at me before getting right to work. The doves dust the fireplace mantel with their wings while the mouse organizes the magazines scattered on the coffee table into a neat stack. I grab the books sitting on the end tables and couch and line them up neatly on the shelves. The lizard grabs the hand broom with her tail and scurries across the orange-tiled floor, sweeping up behind her. I grab the dustpan and clean up the piles of debris.

Finally, the five of us collect odds and ends Rocco and I always leave behind. We toss them on the chair near the fireplace.

"Thank you for all your help." I hold open the bag as each of the creatures takes its fill of the blackberries. The lizard and doves leave through the window; the mouse hurries back under the couch. "A presto! See you soon!"

Weariness tugs at my eyelids as the small bit of magic retreats back to its hiding place. I pop the last of the black-berries in my mouth, letting their sweetness restore my energy. I amble down the stairs to toss Rocco's stuff in his room before heading to mine for the night.

It's not hard separating our things. His are pristine—a navy blue New York Yankees baseball hat, a well-cared-for gray hoodie, and a pair of black slippers. I toss them all in a heap on his bed and bring my stuff to my room, where I throw everything in a pile on the floor.

I stifle a yawn and look over at the alarm clock on my nightstand. It says 9:37 in bright green numbers. Normally, I can stay up much later, but thanks to Rocco waking me up at dawn and using my magic, it might be an early night. Maybe it'll do me some good.

Something on my bed catches my eye. A dinner plate holding a big slice of tiramisu sits on top of my comforter. Next to it is a note written in Rocco's precise handwriting.

Sorry for being a jerk. You may be a goof, but you're not an embarrassment. Let's talk tomorrow morning.
Love,
Rocco

P.S. There's more tiramisu in the refrigerator. All yours.

Tears prick at the corners of my eyes as I hold Rocco's note to my heart. Tiramisu is my favorite treat. He made it just for me. A tear slips down my cheek. An apology is even sweeter when paired with dessert.

I change into my pajamas and eat the tiramisu while watching the storm rage on outside. It's somehow getting even worse. My thoughts turn to that black cat. Just when I'd almost forgotten about him. I crawl out of bed and hesitate by the window, chewing on my bottom lip. He's not going to be out there, is he? In this weather?

My pulse hammers in my ears. With a shaky hand, I pull back my curtains. Lightning streaks through the sky. My shoulders relax. No cat to be seen. Must've gotten tired of waiting on me to do something interesting. Just to be sure, I check the lock on my window—not that I think a cat can open a window anyway—and shut the curtains tight. Without another thought, I fall into a dreamless sleep.

The knocking at my door is so loud it's basically booming against my skull. Sunlight filters into my room. I sit up and rub the bleariness from my eyes. The alarm clock reads 7:30. "Yes?" I mumble.

"It's me," Zia Clementina says. "May I come in?"

"Sure."

Zia Clementina cracks the door open and smiles in a way that doesn't reach her eyes. Something's wrong. "How'd you sleep?"

"Good," I say, frowning. "What's the matter?"

"Have you heard Rocco return? I checked his room, but he wasn't there. Did he already leave again this morning?" She toys with the gold cornicello hanging from her neck. "I had this awful feeling all night. These terrible visions. You know how I get."

I swing my legs over the side of my bed and slide on a pair of slippers. Zia Clementina can see things. She picks up on energies when they're off. Her visions are serious business. "Did you check to see if the rowboat was docked?"

She shakes her head. "I couldn't remember where the grotto's entrance is."

Without saying another word, I'm running down the hall, taking the stone stairs two at a time. My heart's in my throat as I hurl myself through the back door and onto the tiled patio. Rain's drizzling down, and the breeze flies underneath the bottom of my pajama top, but it doesn't extinguish the fear burning me from the inside out. I can hear Zia Clementina hurrying behind me as I pump my legs faster. My feet hit the squishy earth, my calves screaming. Sweat drips from my hairline, down my face and neck.

He shouldn't have gone out in that storm. He should have stayed home, where it was safe. My throat tightens.

I shouldn't have wished for him to disappear.

I run harder and take a sharp left at the large olive tree that sits near the cliff's edge. A set of worn stairs is cut into the cliff, and I stumble down them until the steps turn to sand and a path to the rocky beach below begins to take shape. I skid down the last few feet of the path and tear open a hole in the knee of my pajama bottoms before scrambling to my feet and making a beeline for the hidden entrance to the emerald grotto. I duck down and crouch underneath the small opening.

I put my hands on my thighs and gulp in the wet, salty air. Zia Clementina arrives only a moment later, stopping to catch her breath next to me. Light filters in through an underwater cavity, creating the brilliant emerald hue that illuminates the water and grotto. Lucciole float just above the sea, flitting around one another in intricate patterns. A squeak echoes off the walls. I look back at the entrance.

"What are *you* doing here?" I groan.

The black cat tilts his head at me and meows.

"You know this cat?" Zia Clementina eyes him with suspicion. She makes the sign of the cross over both of us. "He can't be here! Black cats are harbingers of evil. Terrible omens."

The cat's gaze shifts to her, and he meows again, this time a little louder.

"It doesn't matter right now. We need to find my brother."

I keep close to the wall, careful not to slip on the slick stone path, and travel deep into the grotto until a small gray rowboat takes shape in front of me. It's floating right where it should. I turn on my heel. The large sterling silver ladle Rocco invented and the matching sieve and basin are lined up neatly. Even the spider silk fishing net is folded carefully on a nearby table. Lucciole circle the sieve and basin, their soft light glittering against the silver. Everything is in its place.

Everything except Rocco.

A horrible feeling swells inside me. Something's not right. My eyes cut behind me. The lanterns in the grotto are still lit, their flames burning the glass.

"If he was home, he'd have snuffed them out. He never forgets protocol."

The cat circles between my legs, rubbing up against me before prancing toward his tools.

"Rocco?" I call, my voice bouncing back at me over and over like a creature mocking me from the shadows.

There are no sounds or signs that anyone besides my zia and me are in the grotto. The cat puts his paw on my ankle, and I look down. He stands on his hind legs and puts his front paws on the basin's lip. A strange, round thing the size of a small fist sits in the sieve.

*Meowww, mrow, mrow.*

I pick the object up and note its weight in my hands. A giant golden walnut.

The cat purrs, rubbing his head against my leg.

I stare at the bizarre object as reality begins to set in.

Rocco's gone. And a walnut has taken his place.

7

The walnut looks up at me from its place on the kitchen table, shining in the early morning sunshine. It reminds me of something, but I'm not sure what exactly. I poke it with the tip of my pinkie finger and jump back in my seat as it rolls around in a small semicircle before coming to a stop once more.

Rocco couldn't possibly be *in* the walnut. He's too big. But the walnut is the only thing out of place in the entire grotto. Well, that and the—

*Mrowww. Meow, mrow.*

The black cat trots back and forth over the gerberas in Mamma's window box. He stops to paw at the pane.

*Mrow?*

"Shoo!" Zia Clementina slaps a broom against the window glass and scares the cat out of the flowers. He doesn't go far, though, and instead prowls across the balcony. "The black cat's not helping matters. The worst bad luck comes from a *gatto nero*."

My stomach roils with sympathy for the cat. It's not his fault that Rocco's missing. At least I don't think it is. But before I can say anything, Zia Clementina is pulling her hair into a bun high atop her head and grabbing her bright silver- and purple-beaded bag from the kitchen counter.

"Where are you going?" I rise to my feet, the chair scraping behind me.

"First to the Marini house. I'm going to check if they've seen Rocco since last night." She closes her eyes and takes a deep breath in through her nose, slowly releasing it through her mouth. "Then the other neighbors and shop owners. Maybe my terrible feeling is wrong. Maybe he just went right from moon beckoning to run some errands."

"What about the walnut I found? Don't you think it could mean something?" The question seems silly, but I

**100**

haven't stopped thinking it since we tore out of the grotto and back up to the house.

Zia Clementina shakes her head and smiles wearily. "I don't know, Giada. Let me ask around town first. Then we can look into that walnut."

"But what if there's no time?" I come to stand in front of her. My eyes flash to the walnut sitting on the table behind her and the black cat sitting on the balcony far beyond that. My throat goes tight, and the corners of my eyes sting as my next, terrible question comes out in a small voice: "What if he's hurt?"

"Rocco's a strong boy. He's going to be just fine." Zia Clementina pats my cheek, and I see the tears in her own eyes. "Now stay here. Don't go off anywhere. I'll be back soon, and then we can figure things out from there." She glances over her shoulder and glares. "And don't let that cat in here. We're already knee-deep in bad luck."

Zia Clementina gives me one last look before hurrying through the house and up the stairs. I hear the echo of the front door opening and closing before stumbling back over to the kitchen table and slumping in a chair, head in my hands. Madonna mia. What a mess.

The house is quieter than it's ever been. Rocco's absence seeps into every nook and cranny. It slinks up from the floorboards and twists through the stair railing. It curls up with the dust bunnies underneath the couch and reflects off the silverware in the kitchen drawer. I wished for Rocco to disappear. But now his absence is worse than anything imaginable.

*Meowwww!*

The black cat is back in Mamma's flowers and howling like nothing I've ever heard before.

Annoyance pulses in my skull where it clusters at the front, giving me a headache. This cat might not be responsible for Rocco being gone, but he's been on my last nerve for days now. I walk over to the window and yank it open.

"What's your deal?" I shout. "Just tell me what you need. Please! And then leave me alone!"

The cat sits up straighter, his green eyes shining in the sunlight. "Well, that was rude. I understand you're having a bad day, but that's no way to greet your familiar."

"Rude? Rude! You've been following me around like a shadow for days, and *I'm* the rude one? Ha!" I am about to carry on listing all of my problems for him but stop short and stare down at the cat.

The cat talked. He strung together a sentence that I understood like it was Alessia or Mamma or Papa or who-ever talking to me. Not like Tartufo with his blinking or the baby gryphon, whose emotions I felt when we touched. He actually spoke!

My eyes widen as I take in the strange little creature. Except he doesn't *look* strange. Just an ordinary—if maybe a little bigger than average—black cat.

Except that he can talk.

My fingers itch for my vet's log, to take down every single detail of this cat, but now's not the time.

"Why? What?" I shake my head to quiet the millions of questions trying to push their way out of my mouth and choose just one. "You're my familiar?"

"Sure am. Name's Sinistro." He yawns, exposing his bright white fangs. "Who are you?"

"Giada," I answer, before asking my next question: "And you can talk?"

"Not to just anyone. Just you."

"Why? Guaritori don't have familiars." I crouch down in front of him and extend my hand. He leaps up to meet my fingers and lets me scratch his ears.

"Witches and familiars go together like… Well. Cats and catnip."

Then it dawns on me. I remember something my nonna told me a long time ago. About Diana blessing her followers with animal companions. Excitement thrums in my chest, and I squeal, "This is huge! The absolute biggest thing that's ever happened to me! Only Diana's followers have familiars." I gasp at another realization, springing up onto my tiptoes. "She wouldn't have given me a familiar if I was meant to be a guaritrice. Now there's no way I'm taking the oath."

Sinistro moves his shoulders as if he's shrugging and says, "I don't know the details of how this all works. Just that your magic vibes with mine. It called to me from far, far away." He moves his head in such a way that my hand now falls just beneath his chin. "And your magic felt safe. As if I finally found the warmest, brightest spot of sunlight after looking for hours. Don't you feel it, too? Like your magic's whole?"

If he's my familiar, that means our magic is connected. I squint at the cat in consideration and try to focus on my magical core. I draw it from deep in my belly and feel it twist around my heart and thump against each one of my ribs. It does feel stronger and safer. More complete and controlled as it moves through my body. Maybe I was too busy to notice I haven't been nearly as tired after using my magic these past few days.

"Well. I guess you're right. Huh." Out of all the animals that could be my familiar, I was sent a black cat. After the other bad luck that came my way, it feels awfully ironic. Diana blesses her followers with familiars that are like them. I stare at him, watching as his whiskers twitch. It's kind of comforting in a strange way. Maybe Diana knew we needed each other. Two misunderstood individuals that can protect one another.

I lean back on my heels and cross my arms over my chest. "But you were really annoying about following after me. Why didn't you just talk to me?"

"You had seemed so nervous, frightened that I was a black cat. If I wasn't one hundred percent certain you were my strega, I didn't want to scare you any more than I already had." He looks a little sad and guilt stabs at my heart. Then he adds, "I didn't become absolutely positive until these past couple days when things started feeling off."

"What do you mean?"

"The night I found you, I felt something mix with your magical aura. Something ominous. But I didn't come to you right away because I still wasn't sure what that meant."

I think back to the night I first saw Sinistro sitting in the backyard underneath my window. My stomach clenches. "That was the night I spilled the olive oil and salt without reversing the bad luck."

"I've felt that kind of foreboding magic before." He shakes his head, green eyes wide and alert. "It's the Streghe del Malocchio. I believe they've been trying to get your attention with signs of ill fortune. It's their way. And I believe they've taken your brother." Sinistro pushes past me and prances into the house, leaping up onto the kitchen table to circle the gold walnut sitting at its center. "This walnut," he continues, "is the key to their city."

"Wait just a minute." I walk over to him, placing my hands out in front of me. "Let me get this straight. You came here from…I don't even know where…after feeling my magic call to yours. Then, you knew I was your strega after something bad mixed with my magic. And now you're saying that the Streghe del Malocchio are the problem? That they took Rocco?"

"Sì, that's exactly what I'm saying. Except their magic isn't bad per se. Just heavier. Dangerous." He flicks his tail, and his black whiskers twitch. "It all makes sense, does it not?"

**106**

I rub my temples. The headache from just moments ago is now getting worse. "It's just so wild."

"Like I said, I've encountered this kind of magic before." A flash of something fearful crosses Sinistro's expression, but it disappears in only a moment. "When I felt the disturbance in your aura, I was compelled to protect you, which proved to me that you were my strega."

"So the Streghe del Malocchio made me spill the salt and olive oil?"

"It's how they communicate. Through superstitions and misfortunes. They communicate in threes. But since you weren't paying close enough attention, they took your brother."

"Threes? It was just the olive oil and salt."

"You must have had one more sign of bad luck. Likely last night before he was taken."

I close my eyes and think through all the superstitions my mamma and papa have warned me about. After a few moments it hits me. A lump forms in my throat. "His hat," I manage to croak out. "I tossed his hat on his bed after cleaning up last night."

"Oh, that's not good at all. That's a most ominous sign."

"It's all my fault." I grip the side of the table, my knuckles

**107**

turning white. "This whole ridiculous, out-of-this-world fiasco is my fault. I conjured the Streghe del Malocchio. Madonna mia."

Sinistro puts a paw on my arm. "You didn't conjure them. They were trying to get your attention. Maybe even trying to get your brother's attention first if they took him."

Even if the Streghe del Malocchio were trying to get my attention with their signs, I was still the one who spilled the olive oil and salt. I was the one who threw Rocco's hat on his bed. It may not be directly my fault, but they used me to get to him. Anger sparks in my chest and burns through my veins until my entire body is ignited. "They can't take Rocco without a fight. I gotta make this right. I'm getting him back."

"Then you're going to need this." Sinistro bats the walnut, and it spins on its side like a shiny golden top. "The key to Malafi, the city under the world."

I snatch up the walnut and shove it into my pajama pocket before heading for the stairs. Tiny feet hop from the table to the floor, and I turn around, brow arched. "What are you doing?"

"I'm your familiar, remember?" Sinistro exclaims. "I go where you go. Do what you do. And if you're going to throw yourself headfirst into danger, well, I need to be there to keep an eye on you."

"Hmm. Well, I guess that's fine. The more help going up against these wicked witches, the better." I head down the stairs to my room, calling over my shoulder: "But don't get in my way."

"Wouldn't dream of it," Sinistro drawls with what sounds like sarcasm. I didn't know cats could be sarcastic. Though I guess out of all animals they'd be the best at it.

I fling open my bedroom door and toss my backpack onto the bed. Sinistro jumps up next to it and sniffs around, his tail twitching. Ripping open my dresser drawers, I grab every ingredient I can get my hands on and add them to the already heavy backpack filled with a myriad of tonics, potions, and salves. All the things that'll either help in fighting the Streghe del Malocchio or will at least help heal Rocco if he's hurt. An envelope of dried lavender, a glass vial of snail slime, Mamma Gryphon's feathers, an old blush compact filled with rainwater from my metal pails, and four strands of silver unicorn hair Rocco and I collected last summer. A pang twitches in my heart, but I bury the feeling. I can't fall apart now. Not when I need to save Rocco.

For a moment I consider going through the cellar and closets where we store our guaritore supplies, but there's not much extra right now, and a lot of the potions and tonics that are brewing aren't ready yet. Papa, Mamma, and Rocco were supposed to restock this week, but then my parents got called away. And Rocco got taken. Madonna mia, what a mess all of this is!

With a huff, I zip up my backpack and head for my closet to change into something more appropriate for facing down a coven of evil streghe. They probably won't take me seriously in my unicorn pajamas.

"Turn around," I tell Sinistro. "I need to change."

Sinistro closes his eyes and turns around.

I pull on a pair of jeans and a black tank top. Over that, I put on the leopard-print sweater Alessia gave me for my birthday last year, getting the walnut from my pajama pocket and stuffing it in my sweater's. I fish a pair of black work boots—the ones that look just like Rocco's—out of the back of my closet and shove my feet inside. Finally, I grab a black velvet scrunchie from the top of my dresser and flip my hair upside down to collect all of my thick curls into a high ponytail on the top of my head.

"Well, what do you think?"

Sinistro opens his eyes and faces me. "You look like you mean business."

"It's the leopard print," I say with my hands on my hips.

Sinistro jumps off my bed, and I grab my bag, hurrying to the kitchen to fill it with berries, salami, cheese, some anchovies in a tin can, and bread. The tiramisu Rocco made me the other night sits in the fridge, and I take a deep breath.

*No feelings until after he's safe*, I remind myself.

I shake my head and grab the notepad and pen off the counter to write Zia Clementina a quick note:

Zia Clementina—
So, so, SO SORRY for leaving! A lot's happened in the past half hour and I know where Rocco is. Going to bring him home. Will explain when we get back. Don't worry!
Love,
G

"Now," I say, slinging my backpack over my shoulders. "How do we get to the city?"

"There are many ways into the Streghe del Malocchio's

cities. Doors, windows, portals, cracks, and crevices are all over the world." Sinistro stretches out on the floor, behind in the air, arms out before him. "But that walnut is unique to Positano's door. Think about it, Giada. Where have you seen an ugly big old walnut tree?"

Just as I'm about to tell Sinistro we don't have time for questions and riddles, it hits me. That weird, million-years-old walnut tree sitting in the middle of the village. The one I've passed almost every day of my life.

I shudder. Maybe it *has* been watching me this whole time after all.

"Hidden in plain sight."

"The Streghe del Malocchio like being at the center of things."

"Hmm," I muse with a nod. Tightening my ponytail again, I lead Sinistro up the stairs and out the front door, ready to take on the witches who kidnapped my brother.

## 8

We make it to the village square just as the shops start opening up. The walnut tree looms over everything, larger than I remember it. Its dark, gnarled limbs stretch high, cutting through the sky like cracks in a window. A few crisp orange and red leaves cling to the branches, the rest scattered on the bricks beneath it.

What I've always disliked most about the walnut tree is its face. Even though trees are alive, I'm of the opinion that they shouldn't have spooky faces. Deep crevices from centuries of weathering make the trunk look wrinkled and old. Two large knots sit just below the branches, a pair of creepy empty eye sockets that weep shadows instead of tears. And at the trunk's base the tree's roots form a large toothless grin that's twisted and dangerous.

I tear my eyes away from the tree and look down at Sinistro, who is sitting patiently by my feet. "So...this is the door?"

"Kind of. This is la guardia, the guard. Most of the ways into Malafi have one."

"What's he gonna do? Make us answer riddles to get in?"

Sinistro shakes his head. "His job is to stop people from getting into Malafi. But since you have the key, he should let us in without any trouble."

"Hmm. I doubt it'll be *that* easy," I scoff, pulling the walnut from my sweater pocket. "Nothing ever is."

The walnut is almost bigger than my palm. It's also heavier than it was this morning. At least it feels like it is. I hold it between my thumb and fingers, right in front of la guardia's unsettling sneering face.

"What do we do now?" I whisper.

"Get closer."

I shuffle forward just a little and push the walnut out as far as my arm will let me. No way am I getting any closer to him.

"Uh…buongiorno, guardia."

From the corner of my eye, I see some tourists sitting at one of the café's tables. They stare at me with their brows raised, giggling in my direction. Of course I look ridiculous talking to a cat and tree. I already know that. I don't need people making it worse. And I certainly don't need them seeing me do any real magic.

"Hey!" I yell, swatting the air with my free hand. "Mind your business!" I glare at them until they turn back to their coffee and breakfast.

Straightening my shoulders, I raise the walnut higher and clear my throat. "Guardia! Open your door to Malafi."

The wind picks up, ruffling my curls and sending the leaves skittering around Sinistro and me. A rumbling begins in the tree's roots and vibrates from my legs up my spine until my teeth start chattering. I stumble backward as la guardia's black eye sockets glow a threatening red.

Then, as fast as it began, everything stops. It's like standing in the eye of a hurricane. The wind, the grumbling, and the light all disappear. The air is still, but I feel the magic crackling against my skin. And then a rasp, like brittle branches popping in the fire, fills my ears: "To go down, you must go up."

I look up at the tree's mess of crooked limbs. At the highest point on the tallest limb, another red light flickers in a small knot.

"Up there?" My mouth is dry. I swallow hard and look back at la guardia.

But he says nothing, just smirks his ugly Cheshire grin.

"Ugh!" I stomp my foot on the ground and turn to Sinistro. "How're we gonna get all the way up there?"

Sinistro walks back and forth in front of the tree, his tail swishing left and right as he thinks. "The gryphons. Your brother was visiting that pride on the tops of the cliffs on the outskirts of town. I followed him one day when you were at school and met them myself."

My eyes widen as I catch on to his train of thought. "I helped a baby gryphon and her mamma a couple days ago! Maybe they could fly us up to the door. You're a genius, Sinistro."

He sits down and pushes his shoulders back. "Well, I *am* a cat."

"Giada?" I whip around at the sound of my name. Alessia is leaving the café holding a take-out bag. "What are you doing up before eleven on a Saturday?" Her brow scrunches as her eyes dart down to Sinistro. "And why are you meowing at a cat?"

"Meowing?" My gaze darts to the tables of tourists a few feet away, and I lower my voice to a whisper. "Alessia, Sinistro can talk."

"What?"

"He's my familiar. Right, Sinistro?"

*"Familiar?"* Alessia repeats, eyebrows rising into her hair. "You have a familiar? Since when? I saw you yesterday afternoon!"

"This is your friend from the other day, yes? The one with you in the rainstorm." Sinistro walks over to her and rubs against her legs. "Ciao, Alessia."

The crease in her forehead deepens. "You're both just meowing back and forth to each other. Are you playing a game?"

"What?" I look down at Sinistro and back up to Alessia. "No, we're not meowing."

"Sounds like it to me." She shakes her head.

"Whatever. That doesn't matter right now." The adrenaline that propelled me out of bed this morning slams through my veins once more, and I start to pace across the old cobblestones. "Alessia, Rocco's missing! He never came back after moon beckoning last night. Did you see my zia this morning? She was on her way to your house to talk to your parents, but I don't think they'll know anything, and the weirdest part—" I whip the walnut out of my pocket "—is this! There was a walnut left behind in his basin, and I know there's no way a walnut could get all the way down there unless someone wanted us to see it."

"Giada, you're shaking. Why don't—" she begins, but I cut her off.

"Zia Clementina doesn't believe me, but me and Sinistro put it all together." I come to a stop in front of Alessia and take a deep breath. "The Streghe del Malocchio are real, and they kidnapped Rocco."

Alessia blinks, opening her mouth and shutting it as she processes my rant. Finally, she sighs, "Well, what are we going to do to get him back?"

"Wait. You believe me?" I search her face for any hint of a joking smile, but her lips are set in a firm line, and her eyes are determined.

"Of course I do. You're weird, but you're not a liar. Besides, you're my best friend." Alessia shrugs her shoulders. "Now I'm betting we don't have a lot of time. What's the plan?"

She stumbles back a couple steps as I throw my arms around her shoulders and squeeze her tight. "I love you. You're the best friend in the entire universe."

"I know I am." Alessia laughs.

I release her and square my shoulders. "So. The plan is Sinistro and I are gonna go to the Streghe del Malocchio and get Rocco back." I gesture all the way up to the top of la guardia, where the knot in his flimsiest branch glows red. "The entrance to Malafi, the city they live in, is at the top of this tree."

"You're going alone to the Streghe del Malocchio?" Alessia gapes. "Giada! That's a wild idea, even for you. Let me come with you."

I shake my head. "If I lost Rocco *and* you, I'd never forgive myself. It's better that I go alone. If I'm not back by sunset, you can tell my zia and your parents and all the other streghe where I've gone and maybe come rescue us."

Alessia nods. "Okay, but if you're not back the second the sun dips beneath the sea, I'm coming for you."

"Fair. Oh! But keep Zia Clementina distracted until then. I left her a note telling her I'm gonna get Rocco, but I'd rather she didn't see it and know I was gone, too."

"You got it." She places the take-out bag on the ground and then makes a cross in front of me with her hand. Warmth spreads out from my heart to the very ends of my fingers and toes. "For protection. You'll need it. You have your cornicello, sure, but any extra bit will help. Please be safe and come back if there are any major threats. We can figure it out from there if we have to."

"Thanks, Alessia."

"I'm going to bring these pastries home. I'm betting my mamma's been talking your zia's ear off, so she's probably still there. And I'll make sure she doesn't leave anytime soon." She smiles. "Hurry up and get Rocco back."

Sinistro trots toward the road that leads up the cliff and looks back at me, meowing. With one last glance at Alessia, I turn and run after him.

Rocco never told me exactly where the gryphon pride called their home. He never told anyone. But I suppose he wouldn't have noticed a little black cat following after him. Or knew that same little black cat would be able to talk to me. Not that it matters much if Rocco would be annoyed about us intruding on his relationship with the gryphons now or not. My stomach clenches, and I squeeze my fists tight until the feeling disappears. There's no time to cry. Not until after Rocco's safe and back home.

"We're almost there," Sinistro calls over his shoulder. Sweat dampens my curls and drips down my neck. I taste it when I lick my lips. I thank all the gods for giving me the foresight to rub on extra antichafing salve after my shower yesterday. And for wearing jeans instead of shorts. Chubby thighs and uphill climbing don't mix.

We've passed houses, hotels, and rows of parked cars along the twisting, tight roads. In Positano, the roads are so narrow that cars have to pass one at a time at turns up and down the cliffs. Tourists usually panic about it, but all the taxi drivers say it's safer driving here than in New York City. Not that I'd know. I've never left Italy.

The incline levels out as we approach the outskirts of Positano, and the buildings and cars give way to a road with no sidewalk and nothing but a stone guardrail between us and the terrifying drop into the crystal blue sea. On our right is a jagged cliff face dotted with the occasional shrub. Sinistro crosses the road and paces in front of an overgrown shrub bearing small golden fruit.

I hurry across the road after him, keeping an eye out

for any passing cars that might be rounding the corner. "What're you doing?"

"This is the entrance. Scoot behind this bush. There's a staircase hidden behind."

"Ouch!" A branch snags on my sweater, poking my arm. "It's full of thorns."

"Try to avoid them," Sinistro says rather unhelpfully as he ducks under them with ease. I shoot him a nasty look.

"I'm at least—ow!—nine times your—ugh!—your size." I stumble into the small dark stairwell concealed behind the shrub and within the shadows of the cliff. "How would you expect me to avoid them?"

Sinistro shrugs. "Rocco made it look easy."

"Ha! He makes everything look easy. That's his number one annoying older brother power."

Sinistro hops up a few steps and looks down at me, his green eyes flashing in the dark. "You might want to make it brighter. The stairs wind through the cliff, and it's dark the whole way. *I* can see, but I know human eyes aren't as sophisticated as a cat's."

I roll my "unsophisticated" human eyes and rub my hands together, feeling the pressure of magic build between my palms. Light peeks out from my fingers, reflecting off my skin in fiery shades of orange and red. It flickers like the first flames in a hearth, and I knead it like pasta dough until a ball of light forms. I pat it a couple times until the light brightens and stabilizes and then hold it in my right hand, where it glows enough for me to see in the dark stairwell.

Sinistro nods to the light. "That's an impressive spell."

"Thanks. I learned it from one of my family's spell books."

"You taught yourself?"

I shrug. "Yeah, when I started helping nocturnal creatures."

We climb the rest of the stairs in silence, following along as they twist and turn all the way up the cliff. It's not as tall as the 1,927 it takes to get to the top of Positano's tallest cliff, but it's close at 1,842.

Sunshine bounces off the stairwell's stone walls and chases away the shadows. I squeeze my hand and extinguish the ball of light, following Sinistro onto the vast outlook. It takes a moment for my eyes to adjust to the brightness. But when I look up, there's nothing but a thicket of trees and the cliff's edge overlooking the city and sea.

"Where are they?"

"Gryphons are secretive creatures. They protect them-selves from the outside world." Sinistro takes a few steps toward the trees and flicks his tail through the air. Except instead of swaying back and forth easily, it stops. Hindered by something invisible.

Sinistro gets on his hind legs and paws at the invisible wall. "Elder members of the pride use magic to form a shield around their camp."

"Whoa," I breathe, the excitement thrumming in my veins. "How do we get in?"

"Place your hands against the shield. That's what your brother did."

I move forward and hear the familiar hum of magic. Cautiously, I place my left hand to the invisible shield and watch as it ripples under my touch. It's featherlight against my skin as the gryphons' magic pulls slightly against mine.

Without any kind of warning, the shield falls and we're face-to-face with the pride. The gryphons gather several feet away from us, much closer to the trees. They whistle at each other, their call echoing across the cliff.

They're all huge. Mamma Gryphon was big and scary when I met her, too. But she was only *one* gryphon. There's at least two dozen here. Their yellow eyes blink at me. Some of them rear up, expanding their wings to the length of cars. My stomach clenches, and my mouth's as dry as cotton as I do all I can to tamp down the bubbling fear and stand my ground. Distrust shouldn't be a surprise. Most creatures are wary of humans for good reason. But they dropped their shield to let me in, I remind myself, and they are kind to Rocco.

*Chirrup! Chirrup, chirrup, chirrup!*

Piccolina comes hurtling toward me, stumbling over her lion paws as her fluffy eagle wings pick up the breeze. She crashes into my thighs, and I fall on my bottom. The tension from the older gryphons settles a bit upon seeing Piccolina's cheerful greeting.

"Ciao, Piccolina!" I laugh, leaning back on my elbows. She looks down at me from her place sitting on my stomach, her big eyes blinking rapidly. "Have you gotten bigger these past few days? There's no way you could fit in my backpack now."

*Chirrup, chirrup!*

She hops off, and I scramble to my feet as two more gryphons approach. One I recognize as Mamma Gryphon. She's limping slightly, trying to keep weight off her hind leg, but she looks stronger. The bandage I had used is gone now, and in its place is a pink scar that's still fresh but healing nicely.

Mamma Gryphon bows her head, and I curtsy in response, just as we had a few days prior. The larger gryphon next to her does the same, flapping his massive brown-and-white wings in a flourish. They aren't even fully extended, but the breeze still causes me to teeter backward.

The trio stare at me, heads tilted, as a few more members of the pride take interest and start to move closer. I take a deep breath and try tuning in to them. Speaking the same language as animals has never been possible. Until this morning, that is, when Sinistro was speaking to me just fine. But for those who aren't my familiar, I try to find different ways of communication. Like with Tartufo.

Magic, unsurprisingly, is the easiest way. But it's the most difficult spell I've ever tried to master. And takes a patience I don't always have. It's kind of like adjusting the knobs on a radio in search of a new station. Except I'm modulating my magic to find and communicate with theirs. Sometimes it's a snap of the fingers. Other times, there's nothing but static.

Just like with their invisible shield, I feel the gryphons'

magic, pushing and pulling against mine like waves over the beach. Good. I breathe out and plant my feet firmer on the ground. Their magic's blending with mine. They're letting me in. They trust me. As our magic mixes, it pulses just underneath my skin and concentrates in the nerves of my fingertips.

I walk over to Mamma Gryphon and place a careful hand on her back, brushing over the spot where her pearly white feathers give way to fur the color of fried polenta. Calm, hungry, happy—all her feelings wash over me. So close. I push my magic through those to clearer communication. Focusing on a plane where we can understand one another without words.

And then I find it. Similar to when I healed her wound. Not verbal, but a connection that makes discussion possible.

While not necessary, saying what I wish to communicate aloud helps me better center my intentions. "Ciao, Mamma Gryphon," I greet. "It's wonderful seeing you again. How's your leg doing?"

Mamma Gryphon steps closer to me so my cheek is pressed against her feathery neck and her wing encircles my shoulders. Her magic flutters across mine in the slightest of touches. She's at ease. Piccolina's papa has taken over her hunting duties while she rests and gets better. Mamma Gryphon nods her head toward the male gryphon at her side. The one who bowed to me before. Piccolina stands between his giant front claws, nuzzling his leg.

"That's excellent news." I eye Sinistro, who is watching with large curious eyes. "I wish my friend and I could stay longer to chat, but we are in a hurry. You know mio fratello, Rocco? The boy who's been coming here a couple times a week?" Mamma Gryphon nods. "He's been taken by the Streghe del Malocchio, and I need to save him."

Her magic turns to ice and chills my own. It grows erratic. I lose the thread of our conversation, only feeling the dread and panic winding its way through her.

"Hey, hey. It's okay." I refocus on our conversation and continue brushing my fingers through her fur. She turns to look at me, and I don't need magic to see the concern bubbling up above all her other feelings. "It'll be all right. I'm going to get him back."

Mamma Gryphon's gaze falls on Papa Gryphon. She lets out a soft cry, and he moves closer to us, Piccolina on his heels. Papa Gryphon nudges me with his beak, and I feel his magic enter our space. It swirls around Mamma Gryphon and mine, questioning and curious.

"The Streghe del Malocchio have my brother, and I need to get him back," I explain again. "Except the door to their city is far up a walnut tree. Too high to climb. I came to ask if you might be able to fly me and my familiar, Sinistro, up there." A panic I'd been keeping at bay with all my planning and action edges into my voice. "Please. I need to save Rocco."

Papa Gryphon huffs, his breath warm on my shoulder. He'll help us because I took care of his partner and daughter. And because he respects my brother. But he's wary. The Streghe del Malocchio are bad news. Dangerous crones. Enemies of the gryphons.

"I know, but I've gotta save Rocco. You'd do the same for your family."

He looks at Mamma Gryphon and then Piccolina. Papa Gryphon steps away from me and gives a short nod. In one swift motion, he lies down on the ground and waits for us to climb atop his back.

"Thank you! Thank you all so much." I grip the straps of my backpack tightly and hurry toward him when something catches my sweater.

Piccolina looks at me, her eyes filled with worry. Sadness squeezes my heart as I kneel down in front of her and rub the downy feathers on her head. "I'll be okay. I promise. And I'll visit you again. How's that sound?"

She clicks her beak together and then whistles out a melodious tune: *Chirrup! Chirrup, chirrup, chirrup! Chirruppppp!* It's a high-pitched noise that gets the attention of all the gryphons on the cliff. Some return the call as a deeper, cawing sound. Piccolina nudges me with her beak and repeats the sound again.

I lick my lips and put my thumb and forefinger just inside my mouth to whistle the noise back to Piccolina. She hops up and down, nodding with excitement. Now Mamma Gryphon repeats it, and I feel her magic fluttering against mine again. It's a call they want me to know. One that'll bring the gryphons to me if I need their help.

I place a hand on Mamma Gryphon's beak and thank her and Piccolina. Papa Gryphon calls to me. Sinistro's sitting next to him, grooming himself.

"We better hurry up." I scrabble onto Papa Gryphon's back and settle in below his shoulder blades where his wings jut out. "The sun's almost in the middle of the sky, and we've only got until sunset."

**130**

"What did they say?" Sinistro hops in front of me and scoots back until he's secure between me and Papa Gryphon.

"They're worried. The Streghe del Malocchio are enemies of theirs, too."

Sinistro nods. "Not shocking."

Papa Gryphon stands and unfurls his wings. They're larger than those of every other adult gryphon in this pride. From the tip to his body, each wing is roughly the size of a sailboat. I grip his fur just as he starts to flap them, his brown and white feathers oily and gleaming in the sun as he starts running toward the edge of the cliff and the bright Mediterranean Sea a thousand feet beneath us.

*Caw, caw, cawwww!* Papa Gryphon shrieks.

Sinistro burrows closer to me, and his claws stab my hands as I tighten my hold on Papa Gryphon.

The last few feet between the ground and nothing come fast. There's a heart-stopping moment where we're falling through the air. My stomach is in my throat, and I forget the pain of Sinistro's claws. The adrenaline bursting in my body explodes out from between my lips as a shrill scream. And then Papa Gryphon flaps his wings and catches the breeze as he flies us far above Positano, out over the sea where the boats crashing through the waves look like bits of dirt caught in a puddle.

"Sinistro! Madonna mia, Sinistro, this is amazing!" I scream over the beating of Papa Gryphon's wings.

"Absolutely not. I am not looking."

"You gotta see this! I thought cats weren't afraid of heights."

"It's not the going up that bothers us. It's the coming down." Sinistro shudders. "There's a reason we're always getting stuck in trees."

Papa Gryphon glides back over Positano and makes large circles through the sky as he gradually flies lower and lower, homing in on the center of town, where la guardia has lived for centuries. His magic prickles my skin as a barrier passes over the three of us.

"Did you feel that?" I ask Sinistro.

"He must have cast an invisible shield over us so we're safe from being seen."

We're only a few hundred feet above the top of the walnut tree now. Houses and buildings become clearer in their bright shades of yellow, pink, orange, and white. The tops of people's heads are less fuzzy now, too. And the gnarled branches of la guardia look even more twisted from above than they did below.

I fish the walnut, the key, from my sweater pocket and squeeze it in my fist. "Once we get to the branch, how're we supposed to fit in this door?"

"I don't know," Sinistro says.

"What? I thought you knew everything about getting inside Malafi?"

"I know where the door is, not how to use it."

"Ugh. That would've been good information to give me *before* we decided to fly up to it on a gryphon's back."

Papa Gryphon rears up as he gets to the tallest, spindliest branch with the glowing red knot that looks like a demon's eye.

"We need to be careful," Sinistro warns. "Once we leave Papa Gryphon's back, all these tourists below will be able to see us."

I stare down at the square, busier now than it was only a few hours ago when we ran into Alessia. The café is now serving lunch. Tourists are going in and out of shops, arms heavy with bottles of limoncello and gift bags holding glazed pottery. If any of them saw us all the way up in this walnut tree, I'd get in even more trouble with Mamma and Papa. And likely all the important guaritori, for that matter.

"You said this was the key, right?" I wave the big gold walnut in front of Sinistro's face.

"Sì, we need it to get through the door."

"Well then, maybe we just need to treat it like a real key."

I look down at the people underneath us once more. No one is looking up at la guardia's branches. They are all too busy staring at the pretty buildings and climbing bougainvillea. With a shaking hand, I reach through the invisible shield and push the walnut into the knot with the tips of my fingers.

The flapping of hundreds of wings fills my ears. A thorny and crooked magic grasps my wrist, digging into my flesh and deep down into my bones. Before I can scream, I'm being dragged through the tiny knot. I grab Sinistro by the scruff around his neck, and we're yanked from Papa Gryphon's back into the swirling, pitch-black depths of Malafi.

## 9

We're spit onto the very edge of a long, twisting brick road. I land on my back, and Sinistro is splayed out next to me, looking the most inelegant I've ever seen him. I stand on shaking legs and stretch the soreness out of my spine as I glance over my shoulder to see a large walnut door inlaid with ruby eyes of varying sizes. It's suspended several feet above the road, growing out of what looks like a thick tree root.

I squeeze my cornicello. At least I have this and Alessia's blessing for some protection. Rocco had nothing. My heart sinks. But looking out over this strange city, I don't know if I'm much better off.

Being underground, it shouldn't come as a surprise that Malafi's shrouded in a perpetual night that's much darker than our nights up above. Even the thousands of dim flickering lanterns suspended in pitch-black by the walnut tree's massive roots seem to amplify the darkness as they serve as reminders of light. Of stars, of earth.

It's not only the darkness that keeps me on edge. Malafi seems to breathe. Inhaling deeply, the roots shudder and close. Exhaling slowly, they unfurl and scrape across the air. But there's one part of the city that doesn't feel alive. Below the brick road where Sinistro and I landed is the sea. But it's nothing like the Mediterranean Sea I know. Unlike the sea above, this one is completely still. No waves. No tides. It lies flat like the dregs of tea at the bottom of a cup. A neon blue pool illuminated by jellyfish and glowworms that expands far and wide, disappearing in the dark horizon.

And like Positano, the city seems to be carved into cliffs overlooking the sea. Though instead of the many-colored buildings, blindingly white trulli line the rocky shore and go all the way up. Except not all of them are the same size or have the same cone shape that a trullo usually has. Some are so tall they eclipse the trullo sitting on the next cliff above it. Others are squat and wide but still round. All of them, however, seem to have strange symbols carved into their roofs. Beetles, hands, pentagrams, and other markings I can't make out from where I am above the city are painted in bronze and red on every single trullo. I'd need my symbol translator to decode what all of them mean.

"This place gives me the creeps," Sinistro says as he stretches out his back legs. "Let's hurry up and find Rocco."

"You don't need to tell me twice." I rub my hands together and form the ball of light, holding it in my right hand as we make our way down the road.

The road takes us deeper and deeper, winding us farther into the belly of Malafi. A disturbing screeching noise picks up as we descend. It cuts through the stagnant air and rings against my eardrums. Sinistro's tail sticks straight up and fluffs out on all sides. The racket gets louder as we continue on, and I realize it's the sound of violins. But they're not playing in harmony with one another. The melody's discordant, and the strings are all out of tune.

"How can they like this music?" I groan, feeling the beginning of a headache forming at the front of my skull. Of course this trip to Malafi could get worse.

**137**

"It's truly terrible," Sinistro complains. "At least you can cover your ears with your hands."

I hold up my palm with the ball of light. "Not when I need them for other things. Ugh! This place is awful. How do they live like this?"

Sinistro shrugs. "When you're so accustomed to living one way, it's hard to realize there're options. And maybe they don't have any options."

A pang of guilt stabs my heart, and for a moment I feel bad for the Streghe del Malocchio. This is certainly no way to exist. But then I remember they took Rocco, and the guilt morphs back into anger. Anyone who steals my brother can deal with this miserable screeching for all I care. We reach a fork in the road with a tall crooked signpost with about a hundred different wooden arrows nailed into it. Painted on each wooden arrow are names, a series of peculiar symbols, and kilometers. They must be names of different places, but I've never heard of any of them.

*Caw-caw. Caww, cawwwww!*

A large crow lands on top of the signpost and stares down at us with its black shining eyes.

"Ciao!" I wave at the bird.

*Cawwww! Ca-caw, ca-caw, caww.* The crow responds sharply, moving his head from side to side and flapping his wings.

"Uhh..." I take a step back and glance down at Sinistro. "Not as friendly as I'd hoped."

"You expected a Malafi crow would be friendly?" Sinistro shakes his head.

"Should I not have?"

Before Sinistro can respond, two more crows appear. Each one picking a wooden arrow to settle on.

"Oh, look. Now there's a *murder* of crows." Sinistro licks his paw and rubs it behind his ears. "How delightful."

"Now's not the time to be sassy, Sinistro." I spy one arrow pointing toward the white trulli with MALAFI and 0.8 KM written in messy white lettering, followed by what looks like an upside-down tree and three triangles. "Let's get going."

*Caw, ca-caww!*

*Cawwww, caw!*

*Ca-cawwww, caw, caw!*

The crows swoop down from their perches and surround us on all sides. Their nonstop cawing brings three more crows. The six of them chatter before one of the crows flies off toward the largest trullo sitting all the way on top of the highest cliff.

"Well," I start, eyeing the crows with suspicion. "That can't be good."

"Crows love to gossip. They're probably the Streghe del Malocchio's eyes and ears. Those crones will soon know we're here."

"Great. Just perfect."

The crows hop around us, still trying to keep Sinistro and me in place.

"We don't have time for this," I yell over their noisy chatter. "Get outta the way!" I move my arms in sweeping arcs, the ball of light in my right hand catching the crows' attention. We push forward, and they scatter at the last second in a flurry of feathers and screeching.

The crows aren't easily persuaded to leave us alone. Rather, they follow along after us like the strangest group of ducklings I've ever seen. At least they aren't stopping us this time.

"So much for having the element of surprise," Sinistro whispers, glaring over his shoulder at the little pests.

"Maybe it'll be better. Think about it." I gesture in front of us, at the glowing sea and the stark white trulli. "The sooner we get to whoever's in charge—and I'm assuming whoever it is lives in that big trullo the crow flew off to— the sooner we can get Rocco and get out of here. And the sooner I can take a tonic for this terrible headache." I press my fingers to my temple. "This music's awful."

"We just need to have tact."

I scoff. "I have tact."

"You've got a temper, and you're loud. I hardly think those attributes qualify as tactful."

"And you're an annoying know-it-all. Are you sure you're my familiar?"

"Unfortunately, yes. As much as I enjoy our lively conversation, I very much wish your shenanigans would have kept us above ground. Preferably in a cozy house with plenty of fish to eat and windowsills to snooze in."

"Once we get Rocco back, you can have all the fish you can eat."

"Deal."

We soon come to the edge of Malafi, our murder of crows still following behind us. The brick road we've been following splits into three different directions: one following the shore, one cutting right through what looks like the city's center, and the last sloping up the cliff side.

I point to the third road and say, "Let's go up. We need to get to that big trullo."

Sinistro and I climb up the steep road. It levels out after a few minutes and gives a good view. From here, we can see clusters of smaller trulli and a labyrinth of wagons, tents, and tables down below. A large marketplace right on the shoreline. Curiosity makes me want to check it out, but Rocco comes first. Besides, nothing good can come out of a marketplace frequented by the Streghe del Malocchio.

"Well, well, well. What have we here, hmm?" a cloyingly sweet voice calls from up ahead.

Standing in the doorway of a squat round trullo is a squat round woman. Part of her copper hair is pulled into an intricate series of braids and knots that take the shape of cat ears, with the rest trailing so far down her back it touches her heels. A long black caftan covered in orange, yellow, white, and gray fur hangs from her body. Around her neck is a rainbow of braided yarn. In her arms, a white kitten with startlingly blue eyes plays with the necklace, snagging her claws on the soft material and mewing softly.

Uh-oh. Running into random Streghe del Malocchio

was not part of the plan. Clearing my throat, I say, "Ciao, signora. Just passing through."

"Oh, no you don't." The strega tsks and steps directly into our path. Behind us, the crows scatter as a clutter of cats pours from the trullo's narrow door. "You can't pass me by without a proper introduction."

"Umm, okay..." I take a breath to still my agitation and try again in a cheerier tone. "Ciao, signora! We're so happy to make your acquaintance. Unfortunately, we've got important business to attend to and must be on our way. Arrivederci!"

The strega squints at me before shaking her head. "Not you, darling. No offense, but I don't care much about you."

"Likewise," I murmur, glaring at the woman.

But she doesn't hear me. Rather, she places the white kitten on the ground and slinks closer, bending down in front of Sinistro. She smiles wide enough to reveal a set of sharp-looking teeth, and her sugary voice reaches another octave as she coos, "Ciao, gatto. What a lovely thing you are."

Sinistro looks up at me, expression blank, before looking back at the strega. *Mrow?* he responds with a hint of concern.

"Oh, what a sweet bambino. Let me just—" Without asking, she snatches Sinistro off the ground and scoops him into her arms like a baby. "Now, see? Oh, what a good boy. Such a big boy, too. And all this fluff! You'll do very well living with me." She looks over her shoulder at the sea of cats that continue to flood out of her trullo. "And look! So many friends to play with. You'll fit. Right. In," she says, emphasizing each word with a tap of her stubby finger on his nose.

"Giada! *Giada!*" Sinistro's panicked eyes find mine as he twists in the strega's arms. "Giada, do something!"

I follow the strega as she enters her trullo, Sinistro pressed against her chest.

"Hey!" I yell after her, pushing through the cats. The overwhelming smells of salmon and tuna overpower the tiny space, and the rugs, sofas, walls, and ceiling are covered in clumps of cat hair. More cats come down the stairs and walk in from the kitchen. A trio of them sit on a small ice chest in the corner. And one sticks its head out of a cauldron hanging over the unlit hearth, yawning as if it's just waking from a nap.

"Hmm?" She looks around her trullo until her eyes meet mine. "Oh. You're still here. You should probably get going.

They're not going to keep tuo fratello—your brother—around forever."

All previous thoughts fall out of my brain at her words. "What? You know Rocco? You know what's going on?"

She scoffs. "We all do, darling. And we knew you'd come, too." The strega pulls a red ribbon out of a wicker basket sitting by a broom closet and ties it tight around Sinistro's neck. "Such a pretty, pretty boy. Ahh!" she squeals. "I want to eat all your little toes one by one."

"Ackkk!" Sinistro paws desperately at the ribbon. The strega grabs a brush from the basket and starts swiping it across his head. "No, do *not* brush me. I just got my hair the way I like it," he whines. But, of course, the strega doesn't understand. All she hears is his mewing.

I clap my hands, trying to get her focus again, and she turns back to me with a bored expression. "How did you know I was coming?"

"We were whispering to you. And the other families in Positano. But none of you paid us any mind until we took your brother." She rolls her eyes as if all of this information was obvious. "Sending you that key was no accident. And besides, didn't you see the crows, darling? They told all of us you had arrived." The strega turns back to Sinistro

**145**

once more. "But they didn't tell us you'd brought such a precious little bambino with you."

"What do all of you want? Why did you take my brother?"

"You know? Maybe you can be *my* familiar, gatto."

"No! That's not how it works," I yell, tripping over a sleeping tabby cat as I approach her and Sinistro. "You don't just choose for yourself."

"Black cats make the best familiars. They keep the vermin out." The strega whips her head around and levels a glare at me that sets the hairs on the back of my neck on end. "Rats and humans alike."

I curl my hands into fists, accidentally extinguishing the ball of light, and stomp my foot. "You're not taking Sinistro. He's my familiar."

"Sinistro? Ha! What kind of name is Sinistro?" She nuzzles her cheek to his. "This little love is called Pietro."

"Pietro?" Sinistro and I say at the same time.

"Yes, *Pietro*. A real name." She squeezes Sinistro so tight his eyes bulge. "Isn't that right, Pietro? Oh, you're going to get so much tuna. And a tiny bit of cream for dessert."

"As tempting as the offer sounds, Giada, you need to get me out of here."

Panic surges through my body as my heart hammers in

my ears. The strega's cradling Sinistro, spinning through the dozens of cats. She hums an off-key lullaby and doesn't try to harmonize with the terrible violins at all. I glance at her dozens of cats, watching as they follow her every move, and the idea hits me like a brick.

I sling my backpack over my arm, unzip it, and pull out the tin of anchovies.

Sinistro glances at the tin as I tap it with my fingernail, drawing the attention of a few of the other cats, as well. I follow behind the strega as she twirls between the couch and the coffee table, past the ice chest, and in front of the coatrack. The tin can opens with a quiet scrape, and the scent of anchovies overtakes the small room.

All of the cats look my way, heads tilting, tails twitching, eyes widening. Some of them lick their lips; others meow. A gray cat tries clawing her way up my jeans. The strega stops spinning and takes in the uproar. Just as she opens her mouth to speak, I toss the anchovies through the air. The anchovies and their oil land on the strega's head and drip down her face, onto her caftan.

"Aghhhhhh!" she screams. Her grip on Sinistro loosens, and he hops onto my shoulder just as the clutter of cats swarms the strega, climbing onto her back and arms and head to get their share of the fishy, salty treat.

I run for the entrance, fighting against an oncoming tidal wave of cats. Sinistro's claws dig into my back as we hustle through the door and back down the way we came from. Far, far away from the strega and her hundreds of cats.

# 10

"Let's be clear," Sinistro begins as we run back down to the shore. "If someone tries catnapping me again, please act with more haste."

I roll my eyes. "I had the situation under control."

"Clearly."

"Fine. I'm sorry, Sinistro. At least we now know red's your color."

"It most certainly is not. I prefer cerulean."

"Noted."

Sinistro ditched his red ribbon as soon as we were safely away from the strega. We ditched the crows, too.

Well, kind of. Rather than stalking after us, they circle high above, dipping between the roots and lanterns. We pass more trulli, staying closer to the shoreline in case another strega has any bright ideas, while looking for another way up to the large trullo on the tallest cliff.

Streghe mill about, and most of them, surprisingly, ignore us. Every now and then, one will glance from the corner of her eye but will quickly look away and hurry on past. At least some streghe know how to mind their business. The cramped trulli on our right start to spread thinner as we walk farther along, and the road widens to accommodate the booths and tables we saw earlier from above. The marketplace that caught my curiosity.

We stand at the entrance underneath a creaky wooden sign etched with a huge leviathan and a few markings that look like warped versions of stars. I tug at my cornicello, deep in thought. Nerves build in my belly at the idea of walking through such a busy area. But we have to keep moving. I take a deep breath. We'll be fine. No browsing. Just in and out. Easy peasy.

"Ready?" I ask, tightening my ponytail and looking down at Sinistro.

"I suppose."

"You don't sound very confident."

Sinistro looks up at me and shrugs, saying, "Well, are you? After our last, extremely recent encounter, I trust these streghe even less."

I bounce on the balls of my feet. "We don't have much choice, do we?"

Without any more delays, Sinistro prances through the entrance, and I follow after. We get a couple feet in, and it feels like the marketplace has swallowed us whole. Rickety booths and tables cram every inch of available space, and clusters of streghe wander the narrow bit of path there is left, bumping into us from all sides. We quickly find our way to a small corner so Sinistro can jump on my shoulder again. After a few moments of waiting for streghe to pass by, we manage our way back onto the path and flow along with the crowd.

The marketplace has an energy all its own. It's surprisingly not as suffocating as the other parts of Malafi, but still swirls with that dangerous magic. This is the only place so far that I've felt much of a breeze, but it's created by the streghe themselves. Their fast pace up the twisting and turning path kicks up their long cloaks and gowns, creating a tornado effect. My curls ruffle on the false wind, and Sinistro's fur tickles my cheek.

The second thing I notice is the strange sound underneath the whining violins. A hush that rises and falls as the streghe move along, like thousands of voices are murmuring in a round. It's hardly loud enough to discern actual words. Maybe it's a language I don't know. But it's persistent and seems to almost be an enchantment. A chill settles in my spine, and I shake my head to rid it of the creepy thought.

We get deeper into the marketplace, and I realize it's much, much bigger than what we saw from the cliff above. My feet start to ache as we take sharp turns, move in circles, and come out sideways, still following along with the group. As we move, the streghe start paying more attention to us. Rather than a couple subtly glancing our way, more and more begin gawking without any concern for my glares in response. Our presence is wearing thin on them, not as tolerated as it was when we first got to the entrance. Worry churns in my belly. Maybe the crows told them about the anchovies.

I try to avoid any eye contact and instead look between and around the streghe when I can. Over the quiet hush and noisy violins, streghe standing in booths shout about their wares and haggle on prices.

A strega shouts, "Genuine vampire fang! Two varieties. Bloodstained or clean. Price per tooth is thirteen strands of flaxen hair stolen during a full moon. No other offers will be—"

Another strega yells over her, "Yes, they're rare. Phoenix eggs near hatching. And, no, I won't take that as payment. Absolutely—"

"Listen! If you want to travel through the Labyrinth to Olde Yorque, then go ahead. But I know you won't want to. You'll be back to buy this bushel of rotten golden apples from—" Still another strega huffs.

Their voices bleed into the hush as we move past their booths, and I realize it's not exactly an enchantment but a strange rhythmic chatter manifested from the marketplace's hustle and bustle. It feeds the bizarre energy of this place and works as a melodious counterpart to the violins.

A glint of gold catches my eye, and my magic stirs. An inkling of something familiar. I stop walking, disturbing the flow of traffic, and move against the crowd toward an unassuming booth. Hanging from the ceiling are cured meats. Some look like sopressata and salami. Others look like dried toes with neatly clipped toenails and ropes of intestines that I do *not* want to know the source of.

I tear my eyes away before I puke and instead focus on the variety of cheeses laid out on the moth-eaten table-cloth: Gorgonzola with cracks of blue mold breaking up its milky center, Parmigiano-Reggiano the pale yellow of the moon, ricotta kissed with golden honey, and canestrato with a perfect woven rind. A far cry from the disgusting toes hanging just above.

Next to the cheese display is a strega bent over a large silver pot of curds. She's dressed as oddly as all the other Streghe del Malocchio. Unlike the cat strega, this one is tall and spindly like a cypress. A halo of purple curls surrounds her head. Every now and then a tiny bolt of lightning strikes through her hair clouds, quickly followed by the grumble of thunder. Sitting on her crooked nose is a pair of gold half-moon spectacles with green-tinted lenses that clash with her short flared blue-and-yellow sequined dress. I don't know if there's a Streghe del Malocchio city under Milan, but the streghe's eccentric styles rival those seen at Fashion Week.

The strega pulls the stringy white cheese from the pot with a paddle to test its stretchiness. Then, she puts the

paddle aside and starts squeezing and kneading the mozzarella with her hands in the hot water. As she works, I
catch sight of the gold again.

Hanging from her neck on a strand of silk is Rocco's
cornicello.

"Where did you get that?" I blurt before I can stop myself. I lean a bit over the table and take a closer look. The
tiniest marks on its side, Papa's initials, prove it's Rocco's.
"It's not yours."

"I bought it fair and square in this very market, girly,"
the strega grunts. "Worth a pretty penny, too, I'll tell you
that. Six dita del piede! The best ones I had. Plenty of hair
and no toe fungus in sight. If you want it, you'll need to
offer me something of equal value."

"Uh…disgusting." I shake my head and point to the
cornicello in question. "But that's not the point. That's my
brother's cornicello! How'd it get here?"

The strega plops the balls of mozzarella onto a marble slab and starts shaping them into moons in various
phases. "Have you ever lost a sock before, girly? Or perhaps an earring you could've sworn you left on your nightstand before going to bed?" She shrugs while cutting a
piece of the white cheese into a waxing crescent with a

very sharp, crooked knife. "Our crows love bringing us treasures from the world above. All of your lost goods wind up in our marketplaces. It's just the way things are." The strega places the pretty moon-shaped mozzarella on a silver tray. "They must've found it when your brother was taken. But it's mine now."

"What business does a Strega del Malocchio have wearing a talisman that wards against the evil eye? You *are* the evil eye!"

"Giada," Sinistro whispers in my ear. "Don't make her mad."

The strega slams her fists onto the table, making the little moon mozzarellas jump. "Because when *we* wear a cornicello, girly, it gives us strength. All the evil eyes your protection talisman absorbed on your behalf are slowly released into us. It's an incredible power, so it's rare for us to get our hands on one."

"Well, you need to return it. I'm on my way to get my brother back, and he'll need his cornicello."

"Maybe he shouldn't have lost it, then, hmm?" The strega cackles, an awful sound that freezes the magic in my veins. "You know. You're a cute little witch, girly. Round, rosy cheeks. Bright eyes full of hope." She takes a step back, crossing her arms over her chest, and looks me up and down. "Absolutely disgusting," she spits out.

"Just give me back what belongs to my family, and I'll leave all of you alone."

"You really think you have what it takes to face off against our Madre del Malocchio?" She narrows her gray eyes at me from behind her half-moon spectacles.

"Giada!" Sinistro exclaims.

I ignore him and square my shoulders, nodding once. "Of course I do. I'd do anything to save Rocco."

"Hmm. Well then. Let's see about that."

The strega's purple hair lights up with hundreds of tiny lightning bolts, and it grows bigger until her curls practically consume the entire booth. Thunder roars around her head, and her eyes flash white.

Sinistro groans. "Oh, now you've done it. Run!"

She raises her arms high above her head, and her curls transform into massive purple storm clouds of dark magic. She points her hands at me, and the storm clouds set off in my direction.

I start to run, pushing down the narrow path. With my head throbbing, palms and armpits sweating, and pulse beating out of my body, I scramble past booths and duck

**157**

under the feathery collars and large hats of streghe. Most of them put up a fuss as I push through their tight groups, and some even grab on to my arms and backpack, trying to hold me still for my punishment. But I fight them off and keep pressing forward.

"Oh, no. No, no, no. This is bad."

"You think?" Sinistro screams. "I told you not to make her mad. You don't want to make any of them mad."

The storm clouds are persistent and grow larger the longer they chase me. Lightning cracks through the air, followed closely by a roll of thunder. The storm's on my heels, and I don't want to know what dark magic lives inside it.

"What can I do?" I ask Sinistro in a panic. I take a deep breath, wiping the sweat from my eyes as I fight the fear grappling at my rib cage. "How do I stop this?"

"What'd you pack?"

"Madonna mia!" I scream over the chaos. "I don't remember! I can't concentrate on anything with all this noise. Ugh!"

"Well, hurry up and think!"

"I'm trying!" I dive between a trio of streghe wearing matching red pointed hats and chartreuse jumpsuits. A lightning bolt whizzes past my cheek, singeing off a curl.

The scent of burnt hair—*my* burnt hair—fills my nose, and I gag. Suddenly, as if that bolt struck on the recollection itself, I remember:

"Mamma Gryphon's feathers!"

"You can use them to break up the—"

"To break up the dark magic! Yes!" I finish for Sinistro. He moves higher on my shoulder so I can swing my backpack around and dig inside for one of the feathers. "Since the gryphons' powers grant protection, I should be able to use it as an arrow to burst that cloud and scatter the strega's magic."

"An arrow? Not a shield?"

"I need to be offensive and stop the cloud in its tracks, otherwise we won't be able to get very far while propping up a shield." I close my fists and conjure a spell I've only tried once. One that goes beyond the power of creatures, the moon, and the stars. One that directly asks for aid from the gods and goddesses.

I read about it when I first started looking into Diana and her animal-focused magic. It's a spell that takes concentration, urgency, and a clear focus on serenity. A protection spell that calls upon Diana's bow and arrows, granting the spellcaster the ability to use them and guide each arrow to its mark through telepathy. It's meant to keep defenseless or injured creatures safe from intruders. Technically, that's not what I'm using it for, and I pray Diana doesn't become angry with me misusing her magic. Gods and goddesses usually do. But this is an emergency. Another drawback to casting the spell is it depletes your magic quickly and takes rest to recover from. The one and only time I tried it, only a flicker of the bow appeared before I felt dizzy. Hopefully my bond with Sinistro will give me the strength to complete the spell.

The cloud is only a few feet behind us now, but I stop on the path and turn to face it. Digging my heels into the ground, I hold the gryphon feather between my palms and close my eyes. The rush of noise whirls around me, but I focus on my breathing. Letting the violins, the hush of the marketplace, and the grumbling thunder fade with each exhalation of air.

Exhaling the fear of losing Rocco.

Exhaling Maestra Vita chastising me.

Exhaling disappointing Papa and Mamma.

I let go of all my anxiety and picture Lake Nemi. Diana's clear, placid lake made from a volcanic crater. The Mirror of Diana. Sunken Roman ships lie under its calm surface, strife hidden by tranquility. The magic at my core starts to bubble and expand through my body. It tickles just underneath my flesh, and I can almost *hear* it buzzing. Heat collects in my palms, and I whisper the words I memorized long ago:

*Ergo impetrato respondet*
*multa favore ad partes.*
*Cura prior,*
*tua magna fides tutelaque Virgo.*

Shimmering gold stars flutter from between my fingertips and form the shape of a crescent moon. Diana's golden bow. The gryphon feather sharpens, its tip turning silver. The violins stop playing, and the marketplace's hush goes quiet as the streghe pushing and pulling down the path come to a complete stop. I take a deep breath as the magical bow tingles in my hands. I nock the gryphon feather and feel the string of thousands of small stars vibrate as I stretch it back with three fingers. Handling the bow with a gentle but firm grip, I aim for the angry storm cloud of dark magic, which is now only about three feet away.

With a *swoosh*, the gryphon feather arrow is airborne. It arcs over the heads of the streghe, spiraling until it buries itself in the cloud's side. For a moment, everything goes still. The stillest it's been since Sinistro and I got down here.

But then, a shriek. The cheese-making, toe-curling Strega del Malocchio's wail carries over the crowd. The storm cloud rumbles, changing from a deep malevolent purple to a flash of gold. The sound swallows the strega's cries and travels the expanse of the marketplace, burrowing into every shadowed nook and warped cranny.

Gold and silver light bursts from the cloud, and gold stars fall like snowflakes all around the streghe. They get tangled in the streghe's hair, land on their shoulders, and bounce onto the fabric tops of booths before winking out into gold glitter.

I stifle a yawn with the back of my hand, and my stomach grumbles. The magic at my core flickers on and off, an echo of what it was before I conjured Diana's bow. But then something unfamiliar quickly replaces the magic, gnawing at my center, a hollowness I've never felt before. A deep, all-encompassing shame. And rustling against my skull, a soft sigh of disappointment. Diana's regret for letting me use the spell. I squeeze my eyes shut, a wave of nausea flooding my body. The murmurings of a warning. A sharp pain forms between my eyes. The punishment for misusing such a powerful spell will be a harder recovery time. I take a deep breath, praying for forgiveness. I got off pretty lucky. Her retribution could have been worse than this.

Sinistro nudges my cheek with his head.

"Let's get going while they're distracted," he whispers.

I nod and turn away from the scene, pushing through the stunned streghe and farther down the tight path. We pass more booths, some stacked two or three high that can only be accessed by dubious-looking ladders. Scents of anise, patchouli, rotten fish, and a general dusty musk ebb and flow on the air. The marketplace hush returns, spinning around us in a dizzying rhythm. And, after a few minutes, the violins start up their ear-piercing squealing once more. The throbbing in my head worsens, and my eyelids are heavy. With only a small amount of magic available, I'm not in a place to defend Sinistro and myself right now. We need to get somewhere safe before I can rest and eat something to build my magic back up.

A strega wearing a white shift with metal bustles attached to her waist hip checks me, the metal digging into my stomach as I walk. I glare at her over my shoulder, and she returns the look with a pleased smile and a twirl of her finger through one of her French braids.

"Ugh! This place is awful." I push through another group of streghe and take a sharp right as the path turns into stairs for about eight steps and then flattens out once more. "I don't understand them. Why're they so wicked?"

"They may be keepers of the evil eye and very rude, but I wouldn't call them completely wicked."

I arch an eyebrow. "Really? We've just had two not so great encounters with them. You yourself said you felt an ominous aura mixing with my magic."

"Let me try to explain. Their actions can be perceived as evil. They're temperamental and territorial. And the Streghe del Malocchio in Malafi might lean more into those behaviors than others elsewhere. But as a whole they strive for balance, regardless of what means they take to achieve it."

"What do you mean?"

"When the world's scales weigh too heavy on one side, the Streghe del Malocchio try to make it right. Whether that means limiting the malocchio or employing it, they use their magic and position of power to create stability."

"Huh. Why wouldn't they just limit the malocchio so we can have peace and make everyone's lives easier?"

"Because that's not how the world works, unfortunately. If they don't keep things balanced, humans inevitably create discord and strife all on their own, which would lead to much more trouble than we've already seen up above." Sinistro swipes his tail back and forth, tickling the back of my neck. "The Streghe del Malocchio live by strict rules. They never let the scales tip dramatically one way or another."

"That's all well and good, I guess, but how can we use this to get Rocco back?"

Sinistro's quiet for a moment before he responds. "Now that he's here, you can't just take him back. The scales need to stay even."

"You're saying I'll need to bargain for him?" I swallow, my throat scratchy. Anger thrums at my temples, just behind the headache. "I hate compromise. Especially when it comes to Rocco's life. *They* took him. *They* created this whole situation."

"We don't know why they took him."

"Don't be on their side," I snap.

**165**

"I'm not, but I understand their ways. Far more than I'd like to."

I look at Sinistro from the corner of my eye. He's facing forward, perched on my shoulder, whiskers twitching. "How do you know so much about them?" I ask, my voice softer.

He looks at me, his bright green eyes wary. "This isn't my first time under the world."

**11**

The path starts to widen, taking the shape of a bell, and, for the first time since entering the jam-packed market-place, it feels like I can breathe. The comforting scent of sea salt is a welcome change from the assaulting incense, rotten meat, and sweat. My heart leaps as I get a view of the neon ocean. A school of flying fish with iridescent scaled wings skims along the top, and a large orange fin slaps the water, creating ripples on the otherwise still sur-face. The hush starts to fade, pushing the violins to the forefront. Not nearly as nice of a change as being able to see and smell the sea, but the violins are a lot less disturbing than the rhythmic whispers.

Out here, on this side of the marketplace, there aren't many trulli or streghe to be found. And the few that are around don't pay Sinistro and me much mind. But I wouldn't call their disinterest necessarily a good thing. I know they know what happened just now. And probably what happened with the gatto strega, too.

As if on cue, a long, drawn-out *cawwwwww* sets the hairs on the back of my neck on end, and I look up to see that same murder of crows circling overhead once again. My stomach churns, and I pet Sinistro's head for reassurance. They must have lost us when we were cramped like sardines with the streghe, but they unfortunately can see us again.

"I wish they'd just leave us alone," I complain, trying to hide a yawn with the back of my hand. "I'm tired, crabby, and starving. Diana's mad and punishing me for using that protection spell. We need to rest or we'll have no chance of rescuing Rocco." I try conjuring my ball of light. The orange and red flames dance in my palm for a moment before guttering out like a candle doused with water. "Madonna mia. This is a bad spot to be in. And I don't know how long she's going to be upset."

**168**

"Hmm, considering you single-handedly took on one Strega del Malocchio and lived to tell the tale, I'd say you're doing pretty well for yourself. Diana will get over it."

"Yeah, but what happens if I have to take on *all* of them?" Images of Rocco stuck in some dirty trullo alone and scared while a group of Streghe del Malocchio celebrate and laugh bounce around in my head. I squeeze my eyes shut until all I see are bright fireworks of white and green behind my eyelids. "We can't make any mistakes when rescuing Rocco. And we'll need to find a way out of here fast. Because I don't think they'll be happy with us taking him back."

"If you bargain…"

"I. Hate. Bargains." I cross my arms over my chest, stomach grumbling and fatigue pulling at the corners of my eyes. "I shouldn't have to bargain for my brother. He was mine first. And besides. Guaritori can never *ever* make deals with Streghe del Malocchio. That's one of the rules. We aren't allowed to."

"But you aren't a guaritrice. Not really."

"Still."

"Not even a bargain for your brother?" Sinistro shakes his head in response as he trots alongside.

**169**

*Diana, please!* I think, scrunching my eyebrows together. A frown falling on my lips. I feel tears forming, and I take a deep breath. *Please, Diana. I'm sorry for not using your magic in the right way.* The hollowness persists, filling me all the way up my throat. The shame slides between my organs like a serpent, tightening around my magical core and stopping it from filling back up. *I had to get Sinistro and myself out of trouble. Who knows what that streghe's evil cloud would've done to us? I promise I'll learn more appropriate protection spells. Just let me have my magic back.*

My head continues to throb, but the hollowness pulls back. The shame uncoils just a bit. The same murmuring from earlier drifts through my mind. It's sympathetic, but stern. A request to use the right spells. To learn more. To not cross a goddess.

*Thank you!* I think, and the hollowness starts to recede some more. I breathe deeply, willing the rest of the nausea to go away. It, too, starts to retreat, along with the headache and shame, until all that's left is the usual exhaustion and fatigued magic after casting such a strong spell.

The path widens even farther, and the trulli fall away, replaced by craggy cliff sides pocked with emeralds and diamonds as big as my head. The sea widens, too, pooling on a black sand beach. With no moon to create tides, it simply sits atop the shore and collects like raindrops on a window. I sling my backpack in front of me and rummage around. My hand grasps the cloth-packaged salami, and I unwrap it before taking a huge bite. The fat, pepper, garlic, herbs, and red wine all dance on my taste buds, and I can already feel a small bit of magic start to flutter in my belly.

"Here." I tear a smaller chunk off and hold it out to Sinistro. "Have some."

Sinistro sniffs the bit of meat before taking it gently from my fingers. His eyes widen as he licks his lips, followed by a long purr. "That's incredible. I've never had a sausage that tastes so delightful."

I beam, staring down at the cured meat. "It's a Bellantuono secret recipe. We sometimes sell it in the market." I take another bite, relishing the flavors. "It reminds me of home."

"Is it made with magic?" Sinistro asks.

"Not technically. But food's a kind of magic, too, you know? Probably the most accessible kind. Even non-magic folk can create and taste the magic of food. Anyone can be a kitchen witch."

"Do you have any more?"

I laugh, tossing Sinistro another piece. We continue on in silence, snacking on salami as the path twists deeper into Malafi. The magic at my core is slowly returning but isn't nearly where it needs to be. I need to actually sit and rest before we save Rocco. My heart clenches, and I bite my lip to stop myself from crying. I don't want to rest while Rocco's still trapped somewhere. The thoughts of him hurting and all by himself creep up from the shadows of my mind once more, and I shake my head. It doesn't do any good dwelling in my imagination. I need to focus. The sooner I recuperate, the sooner we can get to Rocco.

Just a bit ahead of us is the entrance to a grotto that looks a lot like the one where we hide our boat and moon beckoning equipment. But instead of being illuminated by the sunlight streaming up under the water through crevices in the rock, it shimmers blue with a soft glow provided by the jellyfish and glow fish swimming around.

I look down at Sinistro. "This looks like a good place to take a break."

He follows me inside, away from the crows' probing eyes, away from the streghe. We find a smooth-looking rock near the water to sit on, and I finally let out a long, deep breath. My shoulders sinking down, spine curled over, I scooch to lean against the rocks behind us.

I open my backpack and pull out the bag of blueberries, along with the hunk of fontina and now kind of stale bread Zia Clementina brought with her. Sinistro pokes around the blueberries, eating a few, while I smear some cheese across a bit of the bread with my finger and finish it in one bite.

"Looks good," a voice says from a dark corner near the water's edge. I jump, twisting around and straining to see who's there.

Of course it's another strega. Who else would it be?

I sigh.

"Do you have enough cheese to share?" she asks.

"If you come out of the dark, I'll give you some."

"Fair enough." The strega steps out from the shadows. She's a broad lady with sharp shoulders and a shaved head. She wears a pair of maroon waders, and a diamond-studded fishing net winds around her waist like a sash and is tied into a huge bow on her bare shoulder. Feathered fishing lures hang from her ears, shining as the water's glow catches them. But that's not the weirdest part of her

**173**

outfit. On top of her head is a peculiar hat shaped like a hand coated in silver sparkles.

I gasp as the fingers tap against her sparkly green eyebrows as if waiting impatiently for the fontina. "Well?"

"Uhh…?" My mouth opens and closes, real words difficult to form as I stare at her bizarre hat.

She tilts her head, and the hand scrambles around her scalp to regain purchase. "The cheese?"

"Oh! Y-yeah, yeah, the fontina." I tear a smaller piece of the soft cheese off the larger hunk and stretch out my arm.

Like a spider, the hand scurries down her head, onto her shoulder, and over her arm to snatch up the bit of cheese. It hurries back up to rest on her head, where its slender fingers feed her.

Madonna mia. A frown tugs at my lips, and I thank Diana for the grotto's low light for hiding the shock on my face.

"Mmm. Mmm. *Mmm!*" The strega licks the greasy remains of the soft cheese from the hand's fingers and my stomach turns. "That is some delicious fontina. Grazie, ragazza." She calls me ragazza. Girl. The other two Streghe del Malocchio used nicknames, too. I wonder if they know my name.

"Prego," I say, focusing on her boots.

"So? What do you want from me?"

My eyes snap to hers, and my brows knit together. "Excuse me?"

"You so graciously gave me some cheese, and now I must give you something in return."

"I gave you the cheese because you asked and I wanted to be kind."

The strega raises her glittery green eyebrows as one finger from her hand hat taps her temple. "Oh, ragazza. That's not how things work. Every act of kindness comes with a set of strings attached."

"Why can't I just be kind?"

"Because now there's an imbalance between us. I must repay you in a kindness of equal value."

"Okay…" I look at Sinistro and then back to the strega. "Then I want my brother back. I'm sure you know he's here."

The strega stares at me for a moment before bursting into laughter. The sound bounces off the walls, slapping me in the face from all directions. Anger boils in my chest, and I cross my arms, glaring at her ridiculous hat and her fishing-lure earrings as they bounce with each cackle. Finally, after a moment, her laughter dies. "Ahh, I can't do that for you." Her hat hand wipes a stray tear from her eye. "*Equal* value, ragazza. You gave me some fontina. We want something more for il ragazzo."

"But you kidnapped him! What you and the Streghe del Malocchio did is unfair." I move from my seat on the rock and stomp over to the pretty crystal water. It glitters with flashes of light appearing just under the surface. But the light's different from what the fish and jellyfish produce. The same orange fin I saw earlier cuts through the water and creates waves. I follow the beautiful lacelike webbing of the tail farther up to shimmering orange and yellow scales. And those scales transform into clammy greenish lucid flesh. I gasp as my eyes meet the large pupiled ones of a mermaid.

Madonna mia! I've only seen mermaids from far up on the cliffs. They love the Amalfi Coast. They were born in the Mediterranean Sea before finding their ways to other parts of the world. My veins thrum with excitement, and I'm itching to pull my vet's log and pencil from my backpack and take a billion notes. But that would be tacky. I've only just met her.

She's as beautiful as all the books say. She looks like a woman, but her orange hair hangs from her head like kelp, and her fingers are webbed together with the same intricate lace as her fin. Her eyes are bigger, too, and set farther apart on her head. She also has no eyebrows, and her nose slopes down in a way that makes it look like her nostrils can flutter closed when she's underwater. Her sticky, clammy skin is so pale you can see her green veins and the faint purple of her heart trapped behind a humanlike rib cage. On both sides of her long neck are gills, and, as she smiles, I can see a set of one hundred and seven teeth like I've read about in great detail. Each one sharp enough to tear through a human leg or cut a hole into a ship's side.

I smile back at her in return, edging closer to the water. I love every single thing about her. "You're magnificent."

Another mermaid appears, this one with a purple tail, and then another with a red one. Soon more appear, and the grotto is so bright that I have to squint to see properly. They stare up at me, eyes blinking in a strange pattern.

"They like you." The strega pulls a fishing net filled with what looks like seared thick-cut pork chops. She starts tossing the meat to the mermaids, each one snatching a hunk from the air and devouring it in two to three gulps.

"They probably want to eat me," I muse, but not out of

disgust. Mermaids are marvelous creatures. Even if they prey on humans.

"The mermaids here won't eat you." She tosses a few more pork chops into the water, and there's loud splashing as the mermaids dive for the meat. "In exchange for plenty of pork and a safe haven from humans, they light our sea, which helps our fish and underwater plants thrive." The strega tosses the now-empty fishing net aside and places her hands on her hips. "It's a balanced ecosystem that benefits us all, ragazza."

I dip my hand in the cool water, swirling my fingers in a tight triangular pattern. The magic that's built up in my core starts to prickle, traveling through my veins and buzzing in my fingertips. The water around my hand glows, and I close my eyes, trying to focus on the mermaids' magic like I did with the gryphons.

There's nothing at first. I don't know if communicating with half-human creatures is much more difficult for Diana's other followers or just for me because I already have trouble interacting with humans, but it takes more patience and skill than I anticipated. Likely because their human sides are cagier, not as open.

I roll my shoulders and center my magic further, nudging against the mermaids' minds again. After a moment, their emotions trickle through our faint connection. I can sense that they don't want to communicate but aren't opposed to sharing their feelings. And since my magic moves like an electrical current in the water, I can feel each mermaid's emotions. The magical connection widens as the mermaids become more comfortable. Serenity, excitement, delight, and more flood through and bounce around my body. I pull my hand out from the water and sit back on my heels, grabbing my backpack from where it sits near Sinistro.

I feel the strega's eyes on me and the hairs on my neck bristle.

"But *you all* took my brother." I take the makeup compact of rainwater and a few strands of unicorn hair from my backpack and snatch a handful of pink-and-white spire shells from near the water. Carefully, I soak the shells in the rainwater for a moment before threading them together with the unicorn hair one by one. "We're unwilling participants in this bargain. It seems like you tilted the scales in order to create the balance you wanted."

"Giada, don't provoke her." Sinistro shakes his head from

his spot curled up into a ball. "I don't feel like running away from another strega just yet."

The strega's hat hand turns into a fist as her lips quirk downward. "I wouldn't say that, ragazza. You weren't listening to us when we gave you warnings and struck an initial deal. We needed to take action."

I thread the unicorn hair through the spire shells a fourth time, making sure they're tightly in place, and grab the small jar of snail slime out of my backpack. I add a drop of rainwater to the slime and rub the mixture onto the unicorn-threaded side of the spire shells, adhering the shells and thread together. The mixture hardens and turns the once individual shells into a hair comb.

I lean back over the water's edge and hand the gift to the first mermaid with the orange-and-yellow fin. She lets out a high-pitched squeal that pierces the air before placing the comb in her orange hair, just above her ear. The comb shimmers, its white glow pulsing in tune with her heartbeat. She dives down under the water for just a moment, quickly breaking the surface once more and extending her hand out to me.

The mermaid places an oyster in my hand. Its ridged

shell outlined with grit and sand. I hold it to my heart, bowing my head, and the mermaid bows hers in return.

"A gift of equal value for the one you gave her." The strega stretches out the net that once carried pork chops and attaches it to the sash of nets she wears over her waders. "Do you understand now, ragazza?"

"I get it." I get to my feet and pocket the oyster. "But I'm still not happy."

"We don't ask for your happiness. We ask that you understand," she repeats. Her hat hand crawls back and forth across her head on its fingertips as if in anticipation. "If you venture deeper into the grotto, you'll find a passage that leads up to the same one where you store your family's boat. That is how we kidnapped your brother." Her hat hand points back to the shadows just beyond the strega. "You can leave now, if you want to. You can leave and let us keep your brother forever, ragazza."

There's just a hint of light flickering from the direction her hat hand points. A green ember that twists up from the darkness, causing the shadows. I look at Sinistro, with his eyes on the exit and his head tilted to the side. We could leave. Even though my magic's coming back after resting and eating some food, I'm still tired. My head

**181**

throbs, and there are bruises from where the streghe in the marketplace shoved and pushed against me. Sweat soaks my hair and back.

Rocco could stay here forever with these maybe not so evil, but certainly mean streghe. Sinistro and I could go back up to my family and friends. As much as I love Rocco and want him home, it's not hard to consider how much easier my life would be not living in his shadow. Or being an embarrassment.

I shake my head. It might be easier, but life just wouldn't be the same without him. I love Rocco too much to leave him here with these streghe. He's my brother. He wouldn't leave me behind if the situation were different. He'd be doing anything to get me back. I can't let him down. Even if we don't see eye to eye. He's my family. And family fights for each other.

"No. Absolutely not. I can't let you keep my brother," I insist. "We're on the same page. I'll give you what you want as long as I get Rocco back."

"Excellent choice, ragazza!" The strega claps her hands together, and the hand on her head wriggles its fingers jazzily.

"As if I really had one."

The strega ignores my attitude and continues on. "I'll bring you to Madre del Malocchio at once."

From the corner of my eye, I see Sinistro grimace, and a hole opens up at the bottom of my belly. I swallow, fists clenched at my sides, as I wonder if making a bargain with the streghe—and breaking a guaritore rule—without knowing what they want in return was a wise thing to do.

# 12

It feels like we spend an hour climbing before we make it all the way up to the biggest trullo in Malafi. The trullo sits on the tallest cliff, and it's so big that its peak scratches against the walnut tree's large roots. From up this high the other trulli, marketplace, and sea are just ghostly shadows below. Painted in white on the trullo's roof is a crooked crown atop a large alert eye. The eye blinks, and I take a step back, surprised by the illusion. Or was it an illusion? I shake my head.

Just on the other side of the trullo, near the very edge of the cliff, is a humongous spindly scale. It's made from wrought iron, and at its top is the withered face of an old crone. Her eyes are black diamonds, glinting in the flickering lantern light as she watches over Malafi. The scale's arms are stretched out wide as if ready to snatch us up. And they're slightly unbalanced, with the left about half a foot higher than the right. Piled high in the scales are millions and millions of crystal balls the size of my fist. I inch closer, watching as storms of light swirl through each ball. Names drift across their surfaces: *Angelo Davini, Maria Christina Rossi, Andrea Abruzzo, Carmine Zucco.*

"What is all this?" I ask.

Sinistro stops grooming his whiskers and prances up next to me. "The Streghe del Malocchio's scales. They're used to maintain balance in our world. Each coven of Streghe del Malocchio is in charge of their own set."

"Huh. I didn't know they had actual scales. I thought it was all metaphorical." I want to touch them so badly, but instead I shove my hands in my pockets. "How do they work?"

"When the scales start to shift, the Streghe del Malocchio must rebalance them. Sometimes that involves moving one of the crystal balls to the other scale. They move the balls by using the evil eye. Compelling a person to 'leap' across the scale, to change their current way of

**185**

being, to avoid the bad luck. Or bring it about." Sinistro's tail twitches as he paces back and forth in front of me. "Sometimes, though, the Streghe del Malocchio must take a ball off the scales entirely. I don't know what'll happen, but you don't want your ball to be taken off the scales."

I peek in the basket nestled between the two scales. Fear claws at my insides as I spy a lone crystal ball. Flashing through the dark gray clouds within it is *Rocco Bellantuono*. I shake my head, trying to rid the panic from rising further, and scurry back to the front of the trullo. Nothing in this terrible village makes sense. But once we get Rocco, we'll be gone for good.

The fisher strega nods to me, her hands on her hips as she looks at the trullo's large wooden door. Next to the door a single candle pulses in a waxy lantern. The crows have landed on the trullo's roof and stare at us with their black beady eyes, interested in whatever fate holds for us inside. I take a deep breath, inhaling the last lingering scents of the sea, and look down at Sinistro.

"Are you ready?" I whisper.

He nods. "Are *you* ready?"

I roll my shoulders and crack my knuckles. "Ready."

"Andiamo—here we go—ragazza." The strega raps the

brass Gorgon knocker against the door three times and takes a step back. Her hat hand drums its fingers against her sparkly green brows impatiently. I stand behind her with Sinistro behind me. When all of this started, I never planned on using the front door to rescue Rocco. But here we stand, an unlikely trio politely waiting entrance rather than taking the trullo by storm.

A strega with straight white hair that pools on the floor like a bridal veil pokes her head out from the door. Her thin lips curl into a grin as she cranes her neck to see me.

"Well, well, well…" Her voice is a rasp of grit underfoot. "La piccola strega. The small witch. Come inside. We've all been waiting for you."

The fisher strega looks down at me, her mouth cut in a straight line. She pushes Sinistro and me ahead of her before stepping in after us. The trullo opens up into a giant rotunda with high wood beams dripping with cobwebs and candle wax. Thousands of candles light up the cavernous room, clustered on every visible shelf, candelabra, and chandelier. The round wall is jammed with every kind of door imaginable. Short and wide doors, tall and narrow doors, rectangular doors, circular doors. White, black, red, green, violet, orange. Some upside-down, others on their sides. There isn't any space for anything else on the walls. Just dozens and dozens of doors that lead to who knows where.

I swallow, taking them all in. Rocco could be behind any of them. *Anything* could be behind these doors. Cerberus, a muster of peacocks, or even a totally different dimension. This trullo was set up like an anthill—a series of chambers with one central point and the queen at the middle of it all.

A red-and-golden door in the center of the wall just opposite us swings open, and out walks a strega flanked by the gatto and cheese-making streghe from earlier. "Ciao, Giada!" Her booming voice echoes through the room and smacks right into me. The strega looks at me, chin raised, as she arches a perfectly plucked eyebrow. "I am the Madre del Malocchio. I hope my coven has been good to you."

I leap back, nearly colliding with Sinistro. Madre del Malocchio, the leader of all the Streghe del Malocchio. She stands before me at seven feet tall and wielding a spindly onyx walking cane. Her indigo hair is twisted into large twin horns that curl out from her temples like a ram's, both of them sprinkled with twinkling silver stars. Madre's long, inky black robes billow out behind her as she walks, and I spy a pair of knee-high lace-up combat boots on her feet.

Her black glittery painted lips quirk up as she gets a better look at me. "Oh, Giada. I'm positively tickled that it was you who finally answered our call. I've watched you for some time."

"You've been watching me?" A shudder curls down my spine, plucking each bone like a harp. "Why?"

She clutches the top of her cane—a frizzy blond-haired, blue-eyed doll's head—with talon-like fingers and waves it through the air in a high arc. "Because you're different from the others, Giada. You. Are. Special. You could be one of us. A Strega del Malocchio." Madre raises both eyebrows and throws me a wink. "If you wanted."

"No. I'd never want to be like any of you." I frown. "Take the two streghe behind you. One of you tried to steal my familiar, and the other hurled a curse at us!"

Madre purses her lips and merely shrugs at my outburst. "Too bad. Maybe one day you'll change your mind."

The fisher strega moves from my side and goes to stand beside the cheese-making strega. Now it's five streghe, including the white-haired one that opened the door, looming over us. My heart launches into my throat as I eye Sinistro. I could handle each of them on their own, but not *five*. And who knows how many other streghe are lurking behind the doors and listening to every word, only a call away.

Tension pulls at the muscles in my arms as I squeeze my fists. "Where's Rocco?"

Madre looks at her sisters, tips her head back, and cackles. It's a sound that scratches against my skull. I clap my hands over my ears and clamp my eyes shut. The noise reverberates through my body, snapping my bones one by one and re-forming them into different shapes. Shapes that echo with the high-pitched, milk-curdling cacophony of her laugh. My teeth chatter. My fingers quiver. My toes tremble.

"Stop!" I scream over the sound.

The cackle dies off until the only sound is the ever-present shrieking violins. A strange comfort after that terrible noise. Madre clears her throat while wiping a tear from her eye with one of her long red fingernails. "You'll have to excuse me, dear. I forget your ears aren't yet attuned to Malafi's sounds."

"Where is he?"

"He's here."

*"Where?"* I stomp my foot, impatience radiating off my skin. "I want to see him."

Madre takes several steps forward until she's only a few feet in front of me and taps her cane on a round door I didn't see before, sitting in the marble floor's center. *Tap, tap, tap.* The sound echoes, booming in time with my heartbeat.

"Are you sure you want to see your brother, dear Giada?"

I nod despite suddenly being not so sure after all. A weight sits in my belly, and every hair on my neck stands up straight. I feel Sinistro inch closer to me, and Madre moves back just as the door slides open with a yawning groan.

A large gilded cage twirls up from the cavernous hole at the center of the room. I gasp. It's not at all what I expected.

The cage's floor is lined with a soft fluffy white carpet. Surrounding its walls are overstuffed purple and green silk feather pillows. On a silver platter at its center is a plate of roasted branzino smothered in lemons and capers and a diamond-encrusted goblet filled with white wine. Tucked into a pile of pillows, with his knees bent to his chest and his head buried in his arms, is Rocco.

A sob escapes from my lips, and tears spring to my eyes. He's never looked so small. So exhausted. But the strangest thing is that not one hair is out of place on his head. There are no bruises, no scrapes or blood. Even his normally mud-caked boots appear to have been cleaned and polished. A new wave of dread mounts in my belly. They've been taking care of him. It's almost worse than if he was dirty or uncomfortable. Taking care of him means they've got plans for him.

"R-Rocco?" My voice cracks on his name. He flinches at the sound, tilting his head and peeking through the curtain of hair hanging over his face.

"Giada." He sounds so far away, as if he's whispering from the bottom of a well. My palms sweat, and my throat goes dry.

I rush to the cage and grip the cold metal bars. "Rocco! I'm here to rescue you."

"You shouldn't be here. You shouldn't have come for me."

"Are you okay?" I bite back the sob clawing its way up my throat. "You don't look injured?"

He swoops his hair back with a hand and looks at me. It's then that I see what they put him through. The emptiness in his gaze, his dark brown eyes vacant of any emotion. Not even fear. Just a nothingness I have never seen before. Sure, they've taken care of his body, but the terror they've inflicted on his soul... I take a deep breath, trying to keep the tears from falling. They're destroying him from the inside out.

"You need to leave," Rocco begs.

My face grows hot, and I stomp my foot again as anger swells inside me. "I won't. Not without you. Stop being such a baby, and let me help you."

The Streghe del Malocchio inch closer, straining to hear our conversation. The one with the long white hair even has the nerve to cup her hand around her ear and lean in. I take a step back from the cage, eyes narrowed on Madre, and ask, "How do I get him out of here?"

"Our rules won't let us harm him, if that's what you're concerned about. The scales won't allow it. As you can see, he's well taken care of. Comfortable." A smile spreads across her face, revealing a set of sharp, nasty-looking teeth. "But he's ours now. You can't have him back."

"But you like bargains." I stand on my tiptoes, coming around the edge of the cage to see her better. So I don't have to see that awful hollowness in Rocco's gaze and

I can keep my anger at the forefront. Because anger's the best way to deal with these terrible streghe. Anger's what'll keep us safe. I can't be sad. Not yet. "I can make a bargain."

"Giada! You can't—" Rocco presses his face to the bars, knuckles white as he grips them. "We can't bargain with them."

Madre looks me up and down, hands on her hips. "You're willing, then? Your brother wasn't."

The anger seeps from my veins as fear pools in my stomach. But I can't let them see it. Instead, I cross my arms over my chest and roll my eyes. "Clearly. But I'm not my brother. Just tell me what you want so we can leave."

The four streghe behind her murmur with one another in a language that sounds thick and ancient. One I've never heard before. Madre holds up a hand to silence them, and the room goes still. "We have waited for this moment for some time, so it is a joy that it's finally here. You see, Giada, we have sent our signs to many magical families up above." Madre begins to pace, her cane clicking on the floor. "No one would listen. Not a single soul."

"And so you kidnapped Rocco?"

She shakes her head. "We heard your wish, Giada. You wanted him to disappear, and we were able to help."

"No. Don't you *dare* blame all of this on me." I throw my hands out, gesturing wildly. "You took him because you wanted something. It wasn't my fault."

"Your wish and all your bad luck gave us permission to take him."

"Bad luck you created with your *signs*."

Madre shrugged. "We maintain balance, Giada. We may tip the scales in cases of emergency, but we always make sure things are level in the end."

"I don't like you."

"You don't have to." Madre stops pacing to stand just a few feet before me. "But you do have to work with us."

"Giada," Sinistro whispers. "Be careful."

I look at him, his eyes trained on the streghe behind Madre, and take a deep breath. My hands fall to my sides in clenched fists. "I'm gonna ask one more time. What. Do. You. Want?"

"Giada…" Rocco sighs. He sounds defeated, tired. His voice is a warning. But I ignore him. I have to ignore him if I want to save him. Guaritori may not bargain with Streghe del Malocchio, but Sinistro's right. I'm not *really* a guaritrice.

"We want what you have. Our world is so dark, and the streghe are sick because of it. They ache for the moon. And a sky of stars. We've lived below the earth for as long as time. We've lived with this pain forever. The streghe of Malafi don't want to live like this anymore. We want our tides. We want to feel the moon's light on our faces."

I shake my head. "I can't bring you the moon."

"You know how to beckon its light. Even down here, we've heard of your family's abilities. We hoped your brother would do this for us, but he refuses to cooperate. But you, Giada. You know how to gather the moon's light, too. There's a way for you to bring that light here."

Sinistro rubs his body against my leg, nudging me with his head. "Can you do it?"

I turn my back to the streghe so they can't see me talk to him and crouch down, scratching Sinistro under his chin. "I can moon beckon. Maybe I can even use the light to grow a moon down here. And I can call down the stars to collect their stardust. But I can't bring the whole moon down here. I don't even know if stars can survive underground. They need the sky. Papa once called a sick star down to earth to help bring back its shine, but that was only for a night."

"Trying's the only way to get your brother back," Sinistro says.

I look up at Rocco and see him watching me, eyebrows knotted in confusion. Alessia said when I talk to Sinistro I'm meowing. It must be what he hears. The whole situation would be funny if we weren't stuck underground in this trullo lair. "I'm gonna get you out of here, Rocco. I promise."

"Just don't do anything reckless, okay?" Rocco's grip on the cage's bars loosens, and he sits back on his heels. "I don't want you getting hurt."

"I know what I'm doing."

"Do you really?"

*"Ah-hem."* Madre clears her throat from behind me. I stand up and turn to see the Streghe del Malocchio looming overhead. These nosy streghe. Maybe they wouldn't have to live underground with no moon and stars if they weren't in everyone's business and causing all this bad luck to keep the scales balanced or whatever.

I tighten my ponytail and grind my feet into the floor. "I'll figure it out. I'll help you."

Excited chatter erupts between the streghe, and Madre

holds her hand up to silence them once more. "Very good, Giada. I'm not surprised you see reason."

"Great. Now let Rocco out so we can go."

Madre raises one of her slender eyebrows. The smile creeps back over her lips. "Oh, Giada. You won't leave with him today."

My eyes dart between her and Rocco. "What?"

"He stays with us until you fulfill your end of the bargain."

*Tap. Tap.* Madre taps her cane twice on the floor. A poof of shimmering red smoke appears, and as it dies away, a large brass hourglass sits next to Rocco's cage. Golden sand at its top starts to slowly trickle down to its bottom. "You have two days. If you haven't succeeded in those two days, we will have no choice but to eat your brother's heart and consume his magic."

Panic spikes in my chest and fights its way up my throat and out of my mouth. My scream echoes off the room's walls. I rush to Rocco's side and grapple for him through the bars. "You can't do that. You said you wouldn't hurt him."

"And we won't," Madre assures me. "If you succeed. But you agreed to the deal and tipped the scales. Now they must be righted by you fulfilling your promise. Or there will be punishment for your failure."

My face is wet as I hold on to Rocco's clammy hands. His dark eyes are wide, and a flash of fear cuts through the nothingness. Madre directs the tip of her cane at the cage, and an electric charge runs through the bars, jolting me away and flinging Rocco back to its center. I land on my bottom next to Sinistro. My tailbone stings, and I fight back the urge to groan. These wicked streghe will never hear my pain.

"We're serious, Giada. The Streghe del Malocchio don't play." She points at the hourglass as more sand funnels down. "Your time has already started. Get us our moon and stars, and you'll get your brother back. You have two days."

Sinistro leaps onto my shoulder and nudges his head against my ear. "We need to hurry."

"Be careful, Giada," Rocco calls from his cage. He looks as he did when I first saw him. Head buried in his arms, knees to his chest. I wipe the back of my hand across my face and sniffle. My body buzzes with nerves as I take one last look at him before wrenching open the front door.

As I run from the trullo and back down the cliff, just below the screeching violins, I can hear Madre's terrible body-contorting cackle.

# 13

The sunshine burns after being underground for what felt like days. Sinistro and I escaped through the fisher strega's cave, emerging in the one where we keep our boat and moon beckoning supplies. Of course it was easy for them to steal Rocco away when they have a direct link to my family's grotto. After all this is over, we need to move our hiding spot.

I cup my hands over my eyes, squinting under the harsh rays as we trudge up the cliff to my backyard. We were only in Malafi a few hours. Hopefully Alessia was able to keep Zia Clementina away from our house long enough for her to not know I was gone. We hurry up the stone steps to our balcony, and I fling open the glass kitchen doors. The house is warm and smells like basil and tomatoes. My shoulders slump as the calm quiet washes over me. No violins. No whispers. No cackling. But the calm slips away as dread reemerges, sliding down my spine. There's no Rocco, either.

"Zia Clementina?" I call through the house. "Zia Clementina, are you home?"

Sinistro hops onto the kitchen counter and kneads his paws into the notepad. "Seems like she hasn't been here."

I sigh, opening the refrigerator and grabbing the carafe of basil lemonade made from the lemons in our garden. With no Mamma, Papa, Zia, or Rocco around, I drink straight from the glass container. The sweetness and earthy basil unwind the tension curling in my belly. I drink about half before putting it back and grabbing a bowl from the cabinet and filling it with water for Sinistro to lap up.

"We need to find Alessia and Zia." I replenish our snack supply—more berries and fontina cheese, plus some almonds—before we head out the front door and straight for the Marini house.

The Marinis live about half a mile down the road from us. I hop on my bike, and Sinistro leaps into the basket. The wind whips my hair back as I pump my legs up the small hill. As we crest the top, the Marinis' white house with the bright green vines creeping up its side and the large lemon tree sitting in the small front yard greets us. Alessia's sitting on the steps in front of their melon-colored door, book splayed across her lap, fingers tapping on her knees.

Alessia must hear us because she jumps up, the book falling to the ground in front of her. She scratches the back of her neck where her short brown curls blow in the breeze. "Hey! Is Rocco okay?"

Sinistro leaps from my basket, and I toss my bike into the yard, shaking my head. "He's not home, Alessia."

"What? You left him with the Streghe del Malocchio?" Alessia looks around frantically. She clutches the silver cornicello at her throat.

"I didn't leave him there on purpose." I look down at the mud and grit clinging to my black boots. "I, uh… I—I had to make a bargain with them."

"You did *what*?" Alessia presses the heels of her hands to her temples and groans. "Oh, Giada. You didn't!"

The breeze kicks up and the wind chimes hanging from

the lemon tree's branch jangle. I toe the gravel walkway, kicking a large rock. "I didn't have a choice."

"How's Rocco doing down there?"

"They have him in this plush cage. He isn't physically hurt, but he doesn't seem fine on the inside."

"What a mess," Alessia breathes while making the sign of the cross with her fingers.

"I'm gonna make it right, though." I curl my arms around my torso, hugging myself. "Thanks for keeping a close watch on Zia Clementina." I nod to the discarded book. "What've you been doing?"

She crouches and picks it up off the ground. "I've been reading up on soul-healing spells. Just in case. It's good to be prepared. Did you know prolonged encounters with the Streghe del Malocchio can make you feel intense sorrow? Hopelessness, too." Alessia's eyebrows shoot up, her expression grim. I think of Rocco's vacant stare and shudder. "Soul healing's what I want to specialize in anyway." The tonic Rocco's working on, the one that helps with depression, comes to mind. I almost tell Alessia about it, but then stop myself. The tonic's still a secret.

Alessia tucks the book under her arm and tilts her head. "What do we do now?"

I look up. "*We?* No. You're not going anywhere near the Streghe del Malocchio. You can be lookout again. Or keep researching those spells. We'll need all the help we can get on healing him when he returns."

"Yes, we! I'm not letting you handle this on your own, and I'm certainly not going to keep being lookout. You know I can do more than that. I should've been down there with you to begin with. Madonna mia, Giada. You're facing off against something big, and your brother's in serious danger. You need help."

Alessia's eyes are narrowed as she looks between Sinistro and me. All I can do is nod. When Alessia gets that look in her eyes, you don't argue with her.

"Good. Now. Let's talk to your zia," she says. "She went to the Ferraros' house just a few minutes before you got here." Alessia tugs on a blue sweatshirt that was lying on the stairs and runs a hand through her hair. "You said you tried explaining things to her earlier. Maybe she'll believe you now that you've been down there yourself."

Alessia grabs her bike from the side of the house, and together we ride over to the Ferraros' house. They might not be guaritori, but they're still streghe, and the families of streghe who live up above, regardless of which god or goddess they follow, look out for each other. Even if the Ferraro family is a little strange.

We pedal up to the front of their squat and square blue house and already I can hear Zia's sobs through the open windows. My heart sits in my throat, and I have to swallow back my own sadness. I've only ever seen Zia Clementina cry once, and it was after an argument with my papa. That didn't end well. Hopefully the next time will be tears of relief after we get Rocco back.

Alessia and I lay our bikes down on the brick path leading up to the Ferraros' green front door. It's the first time I've ever been to their house. Usually Mamma, Papa, or Rocco visit with them when they need alchemy work for spells and tonics. Already I smell the acrid scent of melted metal. Overhead, plumes of purple smoke churn out from the chimney. I take a deep breath and knock.

A woman with short dark blond hair and kind blue eyes opens the door. She pushes a set of black-rimmed glasses higher up on her nose and wipes her hands on a pair of paint-spattered jeans. "Ciao, ragazze. You don't know me, but I've heard all about you both. I'm Mrs. Ferraro. But you can call me Ari." She looks at me and a sad smile crosses her lips. "I take it you're looking for your zia, sì."

"Ciao, Ari," I greet. "Yes, Alessia and I are looking for her. It's really important."

"Then please come inside." Ari ushers the three of us into her home and guides us down the stairs to a small living room with bright pink and yellow furniture. A man sits with Zia Clementina. They're holding hands as if for some kind of spell or prayer.

I clear my throat, and the man looks up. I've seen him around the village before. His name's Paolo. His curly red hair is unmistakable since not many people—aside from some of the tourists—have it in Positano.

"Oh, Giada!" Zia Clementina hurries over and hugs me tight. "I don't have any good news." She pulls back and looks at me. Her eyes are glassy, and dry tear tracks run down her splotchy red face. Zia Clementina touches her cornicello and looks over her shoulder. "Paolo and I were performing a spell for safety."

"Zia Clementina, I saw Rocco." I hold on to her forearms, squeezing them gently. "He's safe, but he isn't doing well."

Her eyes widen. "You mean he's home? We need to get back to him! The Ferraros gave me a tincture of an amethyst elixir for recovery." She holds up the glass vial of swirling purple gas. "Is he in bed resting?"

**207**

"No, he's not home." My eyes slide past Zia Clementina to Paolo behind her. I look over my shoulder at Ari and Alessia and then down at Sinistro. He nods to me, urging me to tell Zia what happened. "The Streghe del Malocchio have him. He's in a cage in Malafi, their city under ours."

Zia Clementina takes a step back and makes the sign of the cross. Paolo's fuzzy red eyebrows shoot up into his curls, and I hear Ari gasp behind me. A heavy tension settles over everything, and it's as if I sucked any remaining joy out of the room.

"Are you sure of this?" she asks. "Because you shouldn't say that if it's not true. Maybe you fell asleep and dreamt it? You can't just waltz into the Streghe del Malocchio's world. No one even knows how to get *into* their world."

"No one was paying attention to the signs they were sending us." I gesture to everyone in the room. "They tried contacting all of us through small bits of bad luck. They need our help, and, when all of their signs went unheeded, they took Rocco. Remember when I spilled the salt and olive oil when we were cooking?" Zia Clementina nods, her eyebrows knotted in concern. "Well, those were signs. And then I threw Rocco's hat on his bed and wished he'd disappear." My cheeks flush with embarrassment and guilt.

It's not something I want to admit to, but it's better to tell the full truth than fib to make myself look better.

"Giada!" Zia Clementina chastises. "You can't wish things like that. It's extremely dangerous."

"I know that now!" I shout, tears pricking at my eyes. I feel Alessia put a hand on my shoulder, and the anxiety from this whole mess uncurls in my belly. "Sorry for yelling," I mumble. "I understand what I did was wrong and that it's all my fault. But now I need to get him back."

Zia Clementina looks at me for a moment before putting the back of her hand to my forehead. She tuts. "You're very warm. Maybe you're coming down with something. I'm sorry, Giada, but the Streghe del Malocchio probably haven't taken Rocco. They're real, yes, but they aren't reckless. They're intentional. And they rarely kidnap people from above."

"They're *desperate*. Twisting their own rules to fit their needs. And I'm telling the truth. Look!" I push my hand into my jean pocket for the large walnut. A bit of proof from their world. But my jean pockets are empty. "I've got proof. I just need to find the golden walnut." I search through my sweater pockets. Nothing. Finally, I unzip all the pockets on my backpack and dig through everything inside. No walnut. I drop my backpack to the ground and bury my head in my hands. "Ugh! I must have lost it when Sinistro and I got down there."

"That walnut you were trying to show me earlier? Giada, we don't have time for walnuts." Zia Clementina shakes her head. "I think you need to rest. Go back home with Alessia, and we'll figure this out. I promise we'll find him."

"Why don't you believe me?" I whine. "When have I lied to you?"

Zia Clementina cups my cheek. "Take a nap, amore. This is an adult situation." She looks at Paolo and Ari. "We'll find him. Everything will work out."

"I'm not napping. And I'm not going home." I hoist my backpack onto my shoulder and march back to the stairs. Over my shoulder, I yell, "I'm going to get Rocco."

"Giada!" Zia Clementina calls, but it's too late. If she won't help me, that's fine. I know what needs to be done to get Rocco back.

Sinistro and Alessia follow me up the stairs and out the front door. Alessia has her arms crossed over her chest as we stand by our bikes. "Well…that went great," she says with a frown. "Did you really need to yell at your zia?"

I rub the back of my neck, eyes narrowed against the

bright sun. "I didn't mean to yell at her, but I'm so annoyed! Why won't she believe me? This is important!"

"I believe you, and I'll help you. Just…" Alessia looks into the sky as if it might hold the end of her sentence, choosing her words carefully. "Just take a breather, yeah? Don't get worked up into a tizzy or you'll exhaust yourself. We need all our power to get him back if we're facing the Streghe del Malocchio."

"You're right." I kick a large stone out of the path, and it dings off my bike. "But I don't want to wait. They're timing us. We only have two days to get them what they want."

"You never told me what it is they want." Alessia picks up her bike, and I follow suit. Sinistro walks alongside us as we wheel our bikes down the hill and back to my house.

"They want their own moon and stars. They don't have those in Malafi." A shudder rolls down my spine as I think of the darkness, the loneliness, and the unharmonious violins. "No tide because of it. There's this great big walnut tree, and they hang lanterns from its roots, but it's not like the real thing. So we'll need to gather moonlight and use that somehow to make a moon. As far as the stars go, I was thinking we could fish a few from the sky and bring them down there."

Alessia arches a brow. "Remember what Maestra Vita said, though? The stars can't live on our world for very long. Let alone *under* it. They need the sky to exist." She shakes her head and grips her handlebars tighter. "Plus, think of all the streghe who connect their magic to the stars and use them for guidance and worship their light. A star's energy is sentient, and the connection is strong. If a star dies—" Alessia looks down at the ground, scratching her neck "—the streghe tethered to it could lose their magic."

"I forgot about that." I swallow hard, eyes fixed on the winding downhill road. "Maybe they'll be fine underground so long as they have a moon, too?"

"A moon you plan on growing from moonlight?" Alessia takes a deep breath and blows it out.

I nod. "My nonna had a book on extraordinary and mythological plants. She'd read to me from it, and there's a story about how mini moons grow like grapes on the vine at the edges of Lake Nemi. Their roots dip into the lake and lap up the moonlight. It's the only place where moons grow naturally on earth. Mainly thanks to Diana." My lips quirk into a grin. "But I think it's possible to do so with some nurturing, too. We gotta try for Rocco."

"It sounds a little ridiculous, and the stuff with the stars is definitely risky." Alessia tugs at her curls and squeezes her eyes shut a moment before opening them wide and blinking. "But we need to do it for Rocco."

We walk the rest of the way to my house in silence, and the smile on my lips falters as I think about how Rocco could be doing at that moment. And about the Streghe del Malocchio keeping him captive.

14

We can't moon beckon or collect the stars until nighttime, but that's okay. Alessia, Sinistro, and I have plenty to prepare before then.

We grab my nonna's old plant book from my bookcase. The golden title, *Mythological and Mysterious Plants on This Earth*, glows bright against the fading leather binding. Alessia reads up on how to grow a moon while Sinistro and I gather all the materials needed to do so. We collect freshly spun spider silk from Tartufo and pry open the oyster the mermaids gave me, pulverizing the sparkling pearl it held with a marble mortar and pestle.

Then, very carefully, Sinistro and I remove the loose floorboard under my desk and grab the two large jars I have of water and dirt from Lake Nemi, which were supposedly blessed by Goddess Diana herself. I've had these jars of water and dirt for a while now, saving them for a special occasion. I had to trade for them. Three pots of my antichafing salve *and* a flask of Attacco di Tosse potion, which removes a cough with a single sip, to the shopkeeper in Fornillo Beach who sells trinkets to tourists and magical goods to streghe. I hate making that potion. It's syrupy and made with snail slime, and you have to muddle so much mint. Disgusting. This dirt and water weren't cheap.

With a large scoop, we sift the dirt into a silver canister and then do the same with the water in a separate silver canister. Alessia watches as Sinistro keeps the canister steady while I gently trickle in the last of the water, making sure not to lose a single drop.

"Good job, Sinistro." I scratch him behind the ears, and he purrs before moving over to the spider silk sitting on a pillow next to my bed. We begin to untangle it, one thread at a time, and lay the strands on sea serpent scales that washed up ashore on the beach. The sea serpent scales are a nice bed for spider silk, as they're rough enough to keep them untangled but gentle, too, so they don't break.

"Wow, you're really good with all of this," Alessia remarks. "And you're more focused than I've ever seen you in class."

I shrug. "Because this interests me. I'd much rather spend my time with animals and doing stuff like this than healing people." I look up, face flushed. "No offense or anything. It's just that it doesn't feel right for me."

"No, I get it." Alessia nods. "I was supportive, but still a little skeptical. But you have a familiar who found you and that you talk to. Even if it's meowing. That pretty much seals that Diana's chosen you as one of her own. And seeing you in action…" A grin cracks across her face. "It's really cool."

"Thank you," I say, returning her smile. "You know. I feel the same way about you. Even before we started guaritrice classes, when your zio and my papa would teach us the basics, you were so excited. Remember how you'd sit on the edge of your stool in your zio's workroom, head practically in the cauldron while he was brewing? He'd pull you back every five minutes so you didn't fall in." I laugh, remembering Alessia's eagerness. "You know the ins and outs of every spell and potion, and you work *so* hard. I always wanted to be like you."

Alessia blushes. "You are! Just with a different passion."

She goes back to gently collecting the crushed pearl in a silk-lined satchel and rolling up the sea serpent scales with the spider silk inside while I put lids on the silver canisters of dirt and water. Then we wait, sitting on my bed as we watch as the last golden and orange rays of sun disappear under the sea and make way for a purple, dusky sky.

It's nearly nine o'clock as Alessia, Sinistro, and I run through the olive groves where the Marinis keep their rowboat and tools hidden. Our backpacks thwack against our backs, full of the supplies we collected earlier, as we trot down a rocky hill closer to the beach. Zia Clementina still hadn't returned home by the time we left, and part of me feels guilty for not leaving a note this time. But it also hurts that she didn't believe me. We could've used her help.

I shake off the thought as Alessia's flashlight shines on the rowboat and wicker trunk hidden beneath olive vines. The sound of waves lashing against the rocks and the scent of sea salt call from a short distance away. Above us, the moon and stars twinkle, no clouds obscuring their brightness. It's a good night for moon beckoning.

Sinistro hops into the boat as Alessia and I load it up with the giant silver ladles, the silver sieve, a huge silver pail, a long stardust fishing pole, star lures, and nets made from spider silk. We then get to work dragging the boat over the bumpy, gravelly path. Rocks kick up, piercing us in the shins as we pull backward, zigzagging down to the water. The bottoms of our jeans get soaked as we wade into the sea, making sure the bow doesn't dip below the waves. Then Alessia scrabbles inside, and I move to the stern, pushing it in the rest of the way before hopping aboard myself.

My breath comes in short puffs as I relax onto the wooden seat and wipe the sweat off my brow. We both take up an oar and steer ourselves farther out into the sea, away from the shore. There's a breeze tonight, and the wind kicks up the waves. Water sloshes over the side of our rowboat, and Sinistro hisses, jumping onto the seat next to me. We dig our oars into the choppy sea and push as hard as we can. Rocco never let me steer much. Only a couple times for practice and once for a whole month when he broke his arm. But even those times he was right there with me. I think of his patient instructions and the excitement he had when he'd row himself.

My eyes sting as I remember how rude I could be to him when he was trying to teach me. And now he's gone. Maybe forever if I can't get the Streghe del Malocchio what they want. I swallow back the tears and focus on the warm wooden oar and the way my muscles tense and release with each rotation. All I can do is think of the motions. Of each step that'll bring me closer to freeing Rocco.

All along the Amalfi Coast, people leave their boats floating in the inlets and bays. At night, the boats glow ghostly blues and greens as they bob up and down on the waves. Lanterns left on in case someone needs to get to their boat in the dark. From above, they almost look like the haunted specters of lost fishermen or sailors. But from down here, especially with our flashlights, it's easy to see there's nothing supernatural about them. They're a comfort when coming in from moon beckoning. A reminder that we're not completely adrift on lonely dark waters. We pass by the anchored boats and go farther out where their light, as well as the glittering lights of the city, can't reach us. Out where the moon's reflection has a chance to catch on the black sea.

As the lights fade away, a sparkle of lucciole gathers around our rowboat. Their soft white lights blink just like the stars up above. They zip through the air, following along with us as we row farther out. Lucciole like to fly along when we moon beckon. Usually, on quiet, easy nights, only a few of them follow us. It's not unusual for thousands of them to come with us on nights when the water's choppy or there's rain. Their presence is calming, and they always seem to know when a strega needs a boost of happiness or peace.

A chill picks up on the water despite the sweat still clinging to my hair and the back of my neck. I burrow deeper into my sweater as Sinistro nuzzles closer, kneading his paws into my thigh and resting his head in my lap. Warmth blooms in my chest and buries in the spaces between my bones. Even though we've only known each other for a day, it's like I've known him my whole life. It's weird that yesterday I woke up with no familiar and today he's here. This giant black cat that I'd now do anything to protect. I guess that's the point of a familiar, though. We share a bond. Our magic's connected, and we help each other until the end.

"Turn off your flashlight," Alessia whispers as she clicks

hers off. I do the same, and after a few more strokes of our oars we stop in the middle of the moon's soft glow a mile from the last of the tethered boats. Out here it's dead quiet. Lucciole float around us on the wind, their light mixing with that of the moon. Our sweet little guardians here to keep Alessia and me from getting scared. The waves rock underneath us, and Alessia drops the anchor to keep us in place.

We sit what feels like directly under the moon. Her bright face smiles down on us, and I can feel my magic buzzing to the surface of my skin as it soaks up her energy. Diana's followers get extra strength from the moon. But many different kinds of streghe do, though to different degrees. Even though guaritori get a lot of strength from Apollo's sun, for example, they still benefit from the moon in some ways. For most of us, the moon and stars are life. They bless us with power and rejuvenate our magic.

"Are you ready?" I ask, clicking my nails against one of the ladle's handles. Alessia nods and puts the silver bucket in place between us. I pull out three pairs of sunglasses from my bag and pass one to Alessia before carefully balancing another on Sinistro's ears. After we put the moonlight in the silver bucket and it goes through the sieve, it's way too bright. If you look at it without some kind of protective glasses, it can blind you. We each grab a ladle and simultaneously dip them slowly into the moon's reflection. Carefully, we let the glowing water trickle from the ladle's scoop into the bucket. It tinkles against the bottom like wind chimes. The water shines like diamonds as it pours in a steady stream. We repeat the process over and over until the reflection in the sea fades to darkness and the bucket is filled with the overpowering light of the moon.

Alessia puts down her ladle and rests her head in her hands. "Now the hard part."

"We practiced, though." I put the silver fine mesh sieve over the top of the bucket. "It should be fine."

"I've never beckoned before. I'm just nervous." She scrunches her nose. "What if we do it wrong?"

"Well, we won't do it wrong." I shrug. "Plus, our magic will be more powerful when we do it together. Less risk."

Alessia sighs. "On the count of three, then?"

I nod.

"One…"

"Two…"

"Three…"

We put our palms together over the bucket. The lucciole dance through the air, their light growing brighter as they twinkle and feed into our magic. Sinistro keeps his paws on my thigh, feeding his own magic into the circle we formed. Alessia and I begin the spell, speaking the words at the same time:

Moon in the sky.
Moon at night.
Moon in the dark.
Moon so bright.
Come to us now,
Down below.
Gift us with
Your radiant glow.

Alessia and I continue holding on, our magic humming in time and rotating between us like a Hula-Hoop. Then, our magic peaks, and the water in the bucket rises through the sieve and into the air in glistening beads. One by one, the beads float over our heads and hover over the sea for just a moment before bursting. The water sprays against the sides of our faces and drips down our cheeks. Salt stings my eyes, and I close them, trying to keep my focus on preserving our magical ring. It's a little messy, but we didn't do it wrong. One time, Rocco and I forgot the sieve. And that makes things *really* messy. Without the sieve, the water would all rush up at once and get everywhere. I had swimmer's ear after that time and couldn't hear anything for three days.

"Ugh, this is the worst," Alessia mumbles.

"We just need to hold on until the water's all gone."

"But that could take hours, right?"

"Sometimes. It depends on how fast it works."

I rub my eyes into my sweater, hands still connected with Alessia's, and see her curls are soaked with water and her own eyes are closed. Sinistro, too, is drenched, his thick black hair heavy with the Mediterranean Sea. I try not to laugh at how angry he looks. It's as if he was dunked in the bucket and wrung out.

Sinistro hisses. "I know what you're grinning about, and it's *not* funny."

"Sorry," I say, the laughter bubbling up in my chest again.

"Uhh…Giada?" Alessia's eyebrows are scrunched together as she looks down at the sieve rattling in the bucket. "It's not supposed to do that, is it?"

"… It's not."

The rattling gets louder, and the lucciole zoom closer to us, forming a tight circle as Alessia and I entwine our fingers. Panic edges alongside my magic, and I can feel our power waning. "The moonlight's growing unstable," I warn. "We need to hold on or else it could burst out of the bucket."

"Maestra Vita says the light can blind if that happens. That even sunglasses won't keep us safe."

"Or it'll tip us over into the sea."

Even the lucciole's tranquility can't keep the fear at bay. Sinistro sits fully in my lap and reaches up to place his paws on my arm, pushing as much of his magic into ours as he can. The whole boat begins to rock as the moonlight grows unstable, and I hear Alessia gasp as more water pours into the boat.

"What do we do?" she screams. "If we take on any more water, we'll sink!"

I squeeze my eyes shut and call upon Diana under my breath. I stumble over the words as I speak fast. "Keeper of the moon, protector of animals. Goddess Diana, please let us use some of your light to save my brother. In return, I promise to continue caring for animals who need my help."

The boat continues to rock, and I hear Alessia gasp. I hold on to her hands tighter and try again. "I know I misused your magic before. I shouldn't have. But this is an emergency. I need to rescue my brother. I swear that I'll keep providing for your creatures on this earth."

Finally, after a few final waves crash into us, the air around us stills, and the boat stops rocking. Alessia and I both open our eyes and, keeping our hands clasped, peer into the bucket along with Sinistro. Carefully, Alessia removes the sieve. There's no more water. A large sphere of moonlight, like freshly kneaded mozzarella, sits at the bottom of the bucket. Alessia quickly covers it with a lid and secures the latches on all sides. She grins at me, giving me a high five.

"We did it!" she yells, tossing a fist in the air. "I can't believe we did it! That was so scary for a second, but so much fun!"

I wipe off my wet cheeks and push away the bits of wet hair plastered to my face before taking off my sunglasses. "Your first moon beckoning! Congratulations!"

"My heart's beating so fast," she says, removing her sunglasses and Sinistro's, too. "I want to do it like a million more times."

"Well, now we need to fish for the stars. Surprisingly, that's the easy part."

"How do we do that?"

I grab the long, shimmering fishing pole and prepare the spider silk line with a black ball-shaped lure. "Stars prefer dark places and tend to gravitate to anything that looks like a void," I begin while pressing the rubbery lure onto the line. "They latch on to the lure, and we can carefully pull them down to earth." I gesture to the large fishing net. "If you hold on to that, we can keep them in the net once I tug them down."

Alessia takes up the net, and I stand in the boat, balancing carefully with my legs spread on either side of my seat. While I've never fished for stars before, I've seen Rocco and Papa do it plenty of times. It just takes a little practice and patience. Stars are fussy and like doing exactly what they want to do. Which often means floating and twinkling. Not that I blame them. I'm stubborn, too.

I pull the pole over my shoulder and toss the line. The spider silk stretches through the air and high, high, high into the sky. The spooler creaks and winds nearly down to the tiniest bit of line before the lure lands among the stars. I take a seat, pole nestled between my feet, as we sit and wait for something to bite. After a while, Alessia joins me, and Sinistro curls up by my side for a little nap. It takes about thirty minutes before there's a tug. Carefully, I pull the star down from the heavens, and Alessia catches the bright fiery blue ball of light in the spider silk net. The star bounces around in the net, squealing and wriggling and completely put out. My heart clenches at the possible danger I'm putting these stars in, but then I think of Rocco alone in his cage and settle in with another lure, repeating the process again and again until we have at least eleven stars. That should be enough for the Streghe del Malocchio. They never said how many stars they wanted. Just that they wanted a night sky. And maybe that vagueness will be what helps save Rocco.

Alessia coos at the stars and keeps the net at her feet, careful not to look at or touch any of them in case they blind or burn her. She yawns, stretching her arms over her head. "I think I might need a nap."

"We need to get down to Rocco, pronto."

"Ugh. You're right. Once he's back we can all rest." She sighs, rubbing her eyes with her fingers. "Maybe we can at least grab a snack. Moon beckoning totally drained my magic."

My own stomach grumbles in agreement, and I can feel a wave of exhaustion settle in between my bones as the adrenaline starts to wear off. "A snack we can do."

We pack up the fishing pole, and Alessia pats the top of the bucket before we take up our oars once more, rowing back toward the ghost boats and beautiful coastline as the lucciole float ahead of us, leading the way home.

# 15

It's the middle of the night by the time we return to the grotto where we keep our boat and moon beckoning supplies and head back into Malafi. I guide Alessia down the steep, slippery stairwell, both of us using our light spells, making it easier to see in the darkness. Sinistro hops down the steps ahead of us. His tail flits through the shadows, the white spot at its end acting as a beacon.

"Do you hear that?" he asks, his ears pricking up. "The violins. We're getting closer."

A cat's ears are of course better than those of a human,

but after a few more steps the chaotic pricking of violin strings begins to scratch against the stairwell's stone walls.

I look over my shoulder in time to see Alessia scrunch her nose. "What's that terrible noise?"

"Violins," I say, shrugging. "It's kind of their thing down here. Don't ask me why. I have no idea."

"It's terrible," she complains while adjusting her hold on the net filled with stars. "Like when my cousin Alonzo was first learning to play."

The cacophony grows louder the farther we wind down the steps, and a pit forms in my stomach. I hoist my backpack, now weighed down with moonlight and moongrowing supplies, higher onto my shoulders. My mind wanders to Rocco sitting broken and defeated surrounded by Madre and the other Streghe del Malocchio. I shake my head until the images clear away. There's no use in thinking of him beaten down like that. We need to act, and we can't be distracted. All Alessia, Sinistro, and I need to do is get into Malafi, grow the moon, and let the stars fly up into the sky. Then we can get out with Rocco. It shouldn't be *that* difficult.

We reach the bottom of the stairs and exit into the blue grotto where I met the fisher strega. The mermaids are

**231**

long gone, but the water still glows with eels and jelly-fish. The air is heavy as a thick silence weaves its way out from every stone, puddle, and shadow in the grotto. As we make our way through its entrance, the tension only grows. I crack the bones in my neck with the back of my fist and sigh. Malafi was murky and pulled as tight as its infamous violin strings when I came down earlier, but this feels like something else entirely. Like the entire city is holding its breath, waiting for us to fail.

From my side, Alessia gasps and stops short. She grips my arm, head swiveling from side to side as she takes it all in. "Th-the—" Alessia takes a breath and tries again. "The sky...er...or no sky? All the tangled tree roots and lanterns." She frowns, eyebrows drawn together. "It's so depressing down here. Nothing can grow in darkness or candlelight. No wonder they want their own moon and stars. I'd almost feel bad for them if they didn't take Rocco."

"Yeah, well, you shouldn't. These witches are something else."

"Still..." Alessia squeezes my arm before readjusting her grip on the net of stars and goes over to inspect the illuminated sea. "You need to have more sympathy for others, Giada. They must've been really desperate to take him. Think of how much streghe above depend on the moon, stars, and sun. I don't know what I'd do, as a guaritrice, without Apollo's sunlight."

"I don't have to do anything!"

Sinistro looks up from grooming his whiskers, and Alessia squints, arms crossed over her chest. After a few moments, I hold my hands up in defeat. "Fine. I'll *try* to see things from their perspective. But only after they give Rocco back."

Alessia grins and pats me on the shoulder as she walks back from the sea's edge and past me onto the path. "See? I knew you could do it! You don't have to be stubborn all the time."

I roll my eyes and hurry after her. Sinistro takes the lead, retracing our steps from before as we wind our way up the crooked street past rows and rows of white trulli. We walk in silence, the stars' squeaking and the obnoxious violin chords the only sounds between the three of us.

My stomach keeps rolling over on itself, folding and then flattening like waves eating away at the shore. If we mess this up, Rocco won't come home. If we mess this up, the Streghe del Malocchio might demand even more. I clench my fists until the pain of my nails digging into my flesh shoots up my arms. It'll work. It *has* to.

We get to the largest, tallest trullo faster than I'd like. The same painted eye greets us from the roof. It blinks once, twice, and then glances downward as if assessing. Alessia stares back at it, mouth agape.

"Did you see that?" she whispers.

I nod. "Check out the scales over on the far edge of the cliff."

"Scales…" she trails off. Her curiosity compels her to look, and her eyes grow to the size of saucers as she peeks around the trullo's side.

"Nothing here's normal. Just remember that. Don't let them fool you."

Sinistro slinks between my legs and stretches out his back. "Don't let your temper get the best of you. Stay focused."

"I'll do what I need to do to get my brother back," I vow, squatting down to scratch between his shoulder blades. "But I won't do anything that'll put you or Alessia in danger."

"Much appreciated."

I stand straight and head to the front door before nodding back at Alessia. "Let me do the talking, okay?"

"Fine," she says. "But if things turn upside down, I'm stepping in."

"Things are already upside-down," I mutter with a humorless laugh. Hands trembling, I knock once on the door and take several steps back.

It doesn't even take a second for the door to creak open, and I see the same strega who answered the door before, the one with the long white hair that falls down her back like a bedsheet. She looks me up and down, then peers beyond my shoulder at Sinistro and Alessia. The strega grins, revealing a set of pearly white teeth as she says, "Back sooner than we thought, little one. And with a new friend. Madre will be pleased."

"Sure, okay." I cross my arms, tapping my foot. "Can you just go get her? I need to perform the magic outside for everything to work."

"Such an attitude." The strega tsks. "That'll get you in trouble one of these days, little one."

"Haven't heard that one before. Maybe I'd be nicer if you all didn't take my brother. Go get Madre." Through gritted teeth, I add, *"Please."*

**235**

With another click of her tongue, the strega shuts the door.

I move closer to the cliff's edge overlooking the sea. The scales loom over us, and I swear the old crone's black diamond eyes survey us with interest. My gaze strays to the basket where Rocco's crystal ball sits all alone, and my heart thunders in my chest. I shake off the fear, focusing on the mission.

Alessia and Sinistro come over, and I carefully drop my backpack to the ground, kneeling down on the hard dusty earth. I pull the jar of moonlight from my bag, along with the canisters of Lake Nemi water and soil. Alessia sits beside me and grabs the plant book from her own backpack, turning to the bookmarked page on moon vines.

"Are they going to come out?" Alessia asks as she opens the net of stars to let them bounce around next to us.

"I don't know." I shrug. "Might as well get started."

Sinistro puts his paws on the open book and watches me pull out the silk-lined bag with the crushed pearl and spider silk wrapped in sea serpent scales, plus a few extra ingredients, like the same immortal jellyfish goo I used when tending to Mamma Gryphon, a jar of stardust, and two vials of werewolf saliva. While the book didn't say anything about these ingredients being used to coax the moon vine to grow faster or brighter, my gut and experience make me think they can help. And we're going to need all the help we can get growing a moon underground and away from Lake Nemi.

"First thing we need to do is set up the soil and then pour the water over it. The book says Lake Nemi's waters are still except for when there is a breeze. The mountains block a lot of the wind, but most of it comes from the north." Alessia rubs her chin in consideration. "I'll pour from north to south to replicate the wave pattern." She eyes the canister of water but shakes her head before digging at the rough, rocky Malafi earth with her fingers. Sinistro tilts his head, watching for a moment before joining in and turning up the earth with his paws. "We need to be as precise as possible. The lakeside where the moon vines grow is nearly submerged. I'll dig a hole, fill it with the soil, and then top that with the water." Alessia's eyes meet mine, and she worries her lip. "It won't be perfect, but it's what we can do for now."

"We just have to try," I insist while carefully removing the spider silk from the sea serpent scales and folding the mermaid's crushed pearl into the soft, delicate threads.

Magic heats up my palms, pulsing just underneath my skin, and a shimmer of iridescent light presses between my fingers. It's a binding technique Mamma taught me. One of the first spells I learned. We use it to create stronger bandages infused with healing ingredients. Crushed pearl isn't needed to grow a moon, but its restorative properties will help reinforce the spider silk and, in turn, the moon since we're already trying to make this work underground.

According to the plant book, moon vines grow at Lake Nemi because the strong moonlight there gets caught in the webs that spiders build between low-hanging tree branches. I grab two sticks from my backpack and smear them with the immortal jellyfish goo before winding the bound pearl and spider silk around them, doing my best to create a makeshift web of my own.

A loud bang makes the three of us jump, and Sinistro's tail puffs up like an overly fluffed dandelion. Standing in front of the giant trullo is Madre and the other streghe. My lungs close in on my breath, and I grip the stick in my hand tighter.

Behind them is Rocco's large gilded cage.

"Rocco!" I hurry to my feet and make to rush toward him, when I feel a hand on my shoulder. I turn back to see the concern on Alessia's face as she looks past me at the strange and fantastical group of Streghe del Malocchio.

"We need to keep working," she mutters between partially closed lips. Loud enough so only I can hear. "I don't know if these streghe are as horrible as the fairy tales make them seem—" her gaze flicks up and down over them, and she shudders "—but I don't want to find out."

Madre and the other streghe say nothing but move closer toward us. The wheels on Rocco's cage squeak and groan just beneath the grating violins. From the corner of my eye, I see that two of the streghe—the gatto and cheese-making streghe—are pulling his cage behind them. I look back down just as Alessia and Sinistro finish digging the hole. Alessia dumps the dirt from Lake Nemi into the hole while Sinistro pats it down. She wipes sweat from her brow and then carefully pours the Lake Nemi water on the dirt from north to south, mimicking the waves.

I uncork the vials of werewolf saliva and cringe at the musky, rancid odor. Werewolf saliva has a unique odor, and, like a fingerprint, no two werewolves smell the same. According to the book *Werewolf, Therewolf: A Guide to Werewolves across the Globe* by Doctor Danielle Aubin, they use their scents to mark their homes to keep others away. I frown at the stench and drip it over the spider silk, counter-clockwise, in a circle that represents the full moon, until all the saliva's gone. Because of the relationship werewolves have with the moon and how their howl encourages the moon to shine brighter, I'm hoping the saliva will help our moon grow faster.

I brace my hands on my knees and hold my breath, waiting for a reaction. The circle of werewolf saliva gleams silver for just a moment before settling back to normal, and a smile tugs at my lips. No plumes of smoke. No sparks of fire. No poisonous gas. It's not reacting poorly with any of the other ingredients! The silver means the saliva mixed successfully. I pump my fist in the air. My instincts were right. I *knew* it was a good idea.

Alessia takes the spiderweb from me and buries the clean ends of the sticks in the dirt and water so the web's standing a few inches above the ground. Sinistro pushes the sealed bucket of moonlight toward me, and I gently put his pair of sunglasses over his eyes before securing my own. Alessia does the same before handing me the jar of stardust.

I look at the Streghe del Malocchio, their expressions

showing a mixture of curiosity and hunger, and clear my throat. "Uhh. You may want to turn around for this part."

"You have moonlight in that pail." Madre steeples her long fingers under her chin, and her lips curl up, revealing her pointy grin. "How delightful."

The other streghe shift at the mention of moonlight, and their energy grows more tense. The fisher strega moves forward an inch while the cheese-making strega whispers something to the one with the long white hair. Alessia glances at them before quickly looking back down at the plant book, running a shaky hand through her hair.

Sinistro flicks his tail and tilts his head. I'd laugh at how cute he looks in his sunglasses were it not for our creepy audience and the growing pit in my stomach. "They want to see the moonlight. It's unheard of to have moonlight in their cities and villages."

"If they want to go blind, fine. That's on them."

Sinistro stares at me for a long moment. I toss my hands in the air and turn back to the streghe. "You really can't look at it. You'll go blind. You can see it when the spell is complete." I look at Sinistro and say, "There. Better?"

"Passable." He purrs, cleaning the dirt from between his toes.

I roll my eyes and watch as, one by one, the Streghe del Malocchio turn around to face Rocco. I catch a glimpse of his black hair, greasy and plastered to his forehead, but the rest of him is blocked by the witches. My hands go clammy as I think of him watching me do magic. It's possible he still doesn't think I should be here, saving him. But he's wrong. Maybe one of the only times he's ever been wrong. I clench my hands into fists until I feel my nails dig into my palms. They won't get my brother.

"Okay," I whisper to Alessia and Sinistro. "I'm going to try controlling the moonlight with the stardust and lacing it through the web. Alessia," I say, nodding to the stars. "Can you coax them up into the air above the sea?"

Alessia looks at the stars bouncing next to her. They twinkle in the darkness, far brighter than the lanterns hanging from the walnut tree roots. "I think something's off with them," she whispers.

"What do you mean?"

"They're blinking faster than they do in the sky." Alessia touches her cornicello. "Maybe we should take them back up."

My stomach lurches. I crane my neck to get another glimpse of Rocco but can't see him through the streghe.

"We can't. Not yet." I look at the stars a little closer and time their blinking. Alessia's right. Their light is more rapid than normal. But we can't take them anywhere. This has to work. "They'll be fine."

"Giada…"

"Rocco's right behind them, locked up in a cage." My words sound clogged, trapped behind the lump in my throat. I quickly rub the tears from my eyes and take a deep breath. "If they don't get the moon and stars, they'll eat his heart. We need to do this."

Alessia makes the sign of the cross in front of the stars for protection and nods. "We'll do it."

My hands tremble as I open the jar of stardust. Unlike the stars themselves, stardust doesn't have a light of its own. But it reflects light. It's a silvery ash color and gritty, kind of like coarse ground coffee.

I stand up and sprinkle a bit of the stardust over the web, some of the dust sticking to my sweaty hands. I spread more onto my palms in two large circles like I did with the werewolf saliva.

Alessia taps on the bucket's lid. "Are you ready?"

"Yeah. Do it fast," I say, trying to keep the nausea that's churning in my stomach from spilling out onto the ground.

Like a bandage, Alessia tears off the lid. The ball of moonlight shoots out from the bucket and I close the distance between myself and the light, raising my hands to keep it in place. It crackles with magic, and I feel it flutter against my own like the rapid wings of a hummingbird. The moonlight's more powerful than I imagined. My heart beats hard, and my hands ache as the light draws my magic down my veins and out through my palms. The moon's too powerful for any strega to harness, and its light isn't much easier to use in spells. It's why moon beckoning is so dangerous and unpredictable.

Memories flash behind my eyes. Rocco calling me an embarrassment. My classmates laughing at me in guaritore training. Papa's disappointed face when he gets a call from Maestra Vita about my behavior. The Streghe del Malocchio stealing Rocco. Zapping him of his happiness and hopefulness. Anger builds in my core, flaring against my magic. I dig my heels into the rough ground and push back against the light, trying to gain control. A scream echoes around me, and, with shaking arms, I fight to hold on to my power and guide the moonlight into the spiderweb.

The moonlight warms against my hands and sweat

drips down my neck. I press my palms closer and bend the light toward the web, curling my fingers into the brightness and weaving it through the spider silk. The moonlight lets go of my magic, tangling and re-forming as a ball nestled deep in the web. The sticks holding the web vibrate as the light shudders, illuminating the muddy Lake Nemi water below.

I stumble backward, gasping for breath, hunched over with hands on my knees. My throat itches, beginning to feel sore. Sinistro rubs against my legs and I scratch his head as exhaustion starts to weave between my muscles. I take off my sunglasses as Alessia and Sinistro do the same before we all inspect the moon more closely. It's teeny tiny, but it's already growing a few centimeters at a time. It shines innocently, as if it didn't take nearly all of my magic to control it and stick it to the web. My back aches, and my shoulders slump a bit, but I can't help the smile stretching wide across my face.

"We did it," I whisper. "The magic's working. We're growing a moon vine underground."

"I've never seen magic like that," Alessia remarks, tilting her head to get a better look. "You're really good at this stuff."

"It took everything in me. I feel light-headed now."

"Well, you were screaming your head off," Sinistro says.

I look down at him. "That was me?"

He nods.

"Bellissima! Beautiful, Giada!" I turn to see Madre and the other Streghe del Malocchio staring at us—or rather staring at the small ball of light caught in the spiderweb. Madre claps slowly, her eyes illuminated by the moon vine's silver glow. "Very well done. But we want the *moon*. This is just un bambino."

"It's going to get bigger, though."

"How much bigger?"

"Well…" I scratch the back of my neck, glancing at Alessia. The book said the moons are harvested when they're small and don't grow much bigger than strawberries. They're used by followers of Diana for moon rituals and used in potions for moon-influenced creatures like unicorns and werewolves. "It's going to grow big enough for your sky." It's not a *complete* lie. The moon's already growing, and I added those additional ingredients to help it along. It's an experiment.

"We want it now," Madre demands. "We didn't ask for a moon vine. We asked for the moon."

I take a step closer to the moon vine, putting myself between it and the Streghe del Malocchio. "I can go back up and collect more spider silk to hang it in your sky once it grows big enough. Just give it a chance!"

Madre turns back to the other streghe, and they whisper in a group. Not a good reaction. I clench my jaw, looking at Alessia and Sinistro from the corner of my eye. They seem as nervous as I feel. And the longer the streghe whisper in their circle, the less faith I have in our moon vine. Madonna mia. It seemed like they were excited at first. Why are they so disappointed now?

"Alessia." I tighten my ponytail while watching as the stars' blinking matches the fast beat of my heart. This isn't good. I rush over to them. They're no longer bouncing, but rather floating listlessly just a few inches above the ground. "Help me, please."

"They're hurting, Giada." Alessia kneels down in front of them, running her hand along the light of one star. It flickers on and off, its glow becoming duller with each blink. "If they stay here, they'll die."

"No!" I yell. The Streghe del Malocchio stop whispering and turn back to watch us. "No, they can't die. We need them."

"Something the matter, Giada?" Madre asks, tugging at the blond hair of the doll's head sitting atop her cane. "You seem…upset."

"Nothing's wrong!" But I can't help the way my lips tremble and tears sting my eyes. "We're just prepping the stars to fly into the sky."

"Giada?" Alessia calls from behind me.

"Are you sure?" Madre arches a brow.

"Yes, we're sure. Can you release Rocco now? I'll come back down with spider silk to hang the moon. I promise."

"Uhh. Giada!"

"Just a sec, Alessia." I wave her away, glaring at Madre.

She raises her cane, pointing just over my shoulder. "You may want to listen to your friend, Giada."

I turn around to see Alessia wiping at her face, Sinistro leaning against her side. In her arms is one of the stars, its light faded and its body limp. I scramble over to them and fall to my knees, wincing as rocks tear my jeans and cut through my skin. The tears I was fighting back fall down my cheeks. I place a hand to the star and a sob escapes my lips. The star is cold. It died because of me.

Panic edges its way up my spine. Not only is the star dead, but the streghe all over the world who tethered their magic to it are now suffering. They can feel the loss and the star's pain. They may even have lost their magic. My stomach lurches, and I swallow back the urge to puke. It's all my fault.

"Where is our night sky?" Madre asks. "You told us you'd bring us the stars and moon."

"Stop it!" I scream, face hot as I stand up and scrub the tears away. "Give me my brother back! Right. Now."

Madre shakes her head. "I'm afraid I can't do that. You broke your promise. You *lied* to us." She closes the distance in a few long strides and stares down at Alessia, Sinistro, and me, her lip curled. "You know what this means, Giada."

"No, no, no." I try to push past her, to get to Rocco, but she grabs me by my neck and holds me up. Her fingernails squeeze my throat, and my breath comes in short, choking gasps. My toes scrape the ground, but I can't get any purchase. Alessia lunges for Madre, beating her fists against Madre's back while Sinistro claws at her robes.

Madre tosses me, and I land on my backside, a sharp pain shooting up my spine. She looks at Alessia and laughs her horrible, bloodcurdling laugh. I cover my ears as the harsh noise crawls under my flesh. "Your little friend is so brave," she says with a frown. "But unfortunately, a price must be paid. Balance must be restored." Before Alessia can get away, Madre rips the cornicello from her neck and hauls her up by the arm. She sniffs at the curls on her head and taunts, "I can smell your magic. It's divine."

"Balance?" I drag myself up to my feet and grimace at the bruises forming on my legs and blood dripping from my scraped knees. "You already have Rocco!"

Madre shakes her head sadly. "I don't want to take your friend, but through your failure, you have further tipped the scales." Behind us, the scales creak. Out from the middle of the pile on the left scale floats a crystal ball. The left scale shoots another half foot higher into the air. The crystal ball zips over to Madre, dancing above her head. My heart sinks. On its side twists the name *Alessia Marini*. It flashes away, back toward the scales, and falls into the basket, clinking delicately against Rocco's. Alessia's eyebrows shoot up into her hairline, and she screams. Madre waves her cane, and a gold thread stitches her lips shut. I gasp, jumping forward to chase after them.

"You can't hurt her! She's not part of this."

"By coming here with you, she is absolutely part of this."

"But the scale wouldn't have tipped again if you didn't remove her crystal ball!"

"*You* did this, Giada. You failed. And you failed spectacularly." She shakes her head. "You got our hopes up. How do we know you won't dash them again? How do we know you won't abandon us? Not only that, but you brought another person from above. Another strega! When we only called to you. By doing that, you put my people in danger," she scolds. Shrugging, she adds, "Though I won't be disappointed in the acquisition of more magic." Madre looks over her shoulder, sneering at Sinistro. "You're lucky I think taking another strega's familiar is going too far."

"But taking my brother and best friend isn't?"

"Not far enough!" A peculiar gleam flashes in Madre's eyes. She nods to the other streghe. Lightning cracks in the cheese-making strega's cloudy, purple hair, and the hat hand on the fisher strega's head turns into a fist.

The gatto strega pouts, arms crossed over her chest. "Are you sure we can't take the gatto, too?"

Sinistro hisses, back arched.

"Go," Madre bellows.

The trio of streghe spin on their heels, vanishing in plumes of purple, blue, and green glitter. Madre looks at the remaining strega, with her long white hair. "Bring

**251**

Rocco back inside and prepare more cages." She shakes Alessia like a stuffed animal. "We'll need a few."

"Wait!" I yell. Madre pauses, squeezing Alessia's arm tighter, and squints at me. I press my palms together, trying to summon the magic in my core. But there's no fire. No flame. Not even a bit of kindling to spark. My magic is tapped after creating the moon vine. My body's too sore, and I'm too tired to fight back. But I can feel the anger burning a path through my body, exploding from my veins and coiling tight in my belly.

I leap at Madre's back, but she's too fast and blasts me into the air with the tip of her cane. I land on my backpack, coughing up a shuddering breath as the bag digs into my lungs. Sinistro puts his paws on my chest and looks between me and the remaining stars.

"You can't fight her with your fists," he says. "We need to leave. Now."

Madre follows Rocco's slow-moving cage back to the trullo and pauses at the front door. She looks down at Alessia and then back to me, announcing, "You have one day left to save them. Or else."

With that, she tosses Alessia inside the trullo and slams

the door shut behind her. Sinistro forces me to stand. "We need to get the stars out of here. Hurry up!" he yells.

I grip my cornicello, knuckles turning white as fresh tears roll down my cheeks.

The moon vine glows bright in the darkness, now the size of a cantaloupe. Sinistro ushers the quickly fading stars down the cliff toward the grotto. With one last look at the trullo, I run after Sinistro and the stars, my failure replaying over and over in my head.

# 16

Pink, purple, and orange fingers of light bruise the early morning sky. Sinistro leads the stars along the rocky beach, coaxing them to float with his tail. They bolt high above us, their blinking slower and brighter now that they're no longer underground. Sinistro and I watch as they become nothing more than glittering specks of dust over the sunrise.

I rub my palms against my eyes until I see bursts of light. My entire body burns as if every bone in my body was broken and put together in a crooked and incorrect replica of a human skeleton. Nothing feels right, and, worst of all, I used up every last bit of my magic. Not even a kindling potion could rouse the dried-up twigs at my core to spark back to life. I look at Sinistro and catch him mid-yawn. While there's magic crackling off his whiskers and fur, it's not nearly as electrifying as it was when we went down to Malafi. We need real rest and food if we're going to recover. But lying around and eating feels a lot like guilt when Rocco and Alessia are trapped by the Streghe del Malocchio.

One day left. If I don't succeed before then, they'll be devoured.

Tears well up in my eyes, and I swallow them back. "Let's get some breakfast," I say to Sinistro.

"And devise a plan?" he asks, trotting ahead of me up the path to the house.

"And devise a plan." I trudge behind him, wincing as my thighs chafe even despite my salve *and* jeans. It's going to be one of those days.

Light pools from my house's windows, and hope twitches in my heart. Zia Clementina! She can help sort out this mess. I rub my nose and run the rest of the way up the stairs to the balcony, Sinistro close behind. Flinging open the doors, I run through the kitchen.

"Zia! Ziaaaaa!"

Silence.

"Zia Clementina! Where are you?"

No Zia. My own voice bounces back to me.

I rush up the stairs to the front door. My blood rushes in my ears, eyes darting between the open door and Mamma and Papa's bags sitting together in the small entryway. Madonna mia. I tug at my cornicello.

"Mamma! Papa!" I cry, new tears springing forth. They fall before I can stop them. "Zia!" I run back down the stairs to see Sinistro looking up at me from the bottom. "Check out front for them, please? Maybe they're looking for us."

"Giada," Sinistro begins. "I'm not sure—"

"Just check!" I squeeze my eyes shut, jaw clenched. I can't hear him say it. The thing we're both thinking. "Please."

Sinistro passes me on the stairs as I head back to the kitchen, hoping Zia Clementina maybe returned home and at least saw the note I left.

*Drip. Drip. Drip.*

A noise that, in my excitement, I didn't hear the first time I tore through the kitchen.

The walls, the cabinets, the counters. Every inch of the

kitchen is coated in a thick layer of olive oil. It slides down to the floor in streams, slicking the tiles in heavy puddles. The scent catches in my nose and makes my stomach turn. I take a step closer to where Zia's note still sits untouched, now plastered with oil. Salt's sprinkled everywhere in haphazard piles.

I brace myself against the slippery, slimy counters. A scream explodes from my lungs and burns my throat raw. The tears are hot against my cheeks. Blood throbs against my skull, and I press an olive oil–smeared hand to my temple.

They actually did it. Did what I knew they would but didn't want to believe.

The Streghe del Malocchio took my parents and zia.

Madonna mia.

I slide down the cabinet, curl my legs up to my chest, and bury my head in my knees. Tears mix with the oil. So much olive oil. Now all over my hands, face, and clothes. This time, their message wasn't so subtle.

Sinistro kneads his tiny paws on my arm and nuzzles his way into the crook of my elbow. I cry even harder as he pushes what remains of his magic against my core. We sit like that for some time, Sinistro cradled in my arms, my sobs the only sound. My house has never been this quiet. Loneliness gnaws at my bones. A dull, empty pain that makes the bruises and scrapes on my body feel like nothing. I squeeze Sinistro harder.

Rocco, Alessia, Zia, Mamma, and Papa. All gone. Ripped away. Their fate determined by whether or not I can make good on what the Streghe del Malocchio want. My breath gets stuck in my throat, and I beat a fist into the puddle by my side. These terrible, horrible streghe. I don't *care* that they maintain balance in the world. Taking everyone I love so I do what they want is unfair. If they had just asked directly instead of kidnapping my brother and leaving cryptic clues, I would have helped.

"This is ridiculous, Sinistro," I complain. "How'd Madre take them? They should have been protected by their cornicelli. But then she ripped Alessia's right off her."

Sinistro thinks for a moment before saying, "You saw the strega in the marketplace. She was wearing your brother's. It gave her strength. Perhaps their protective powers are weakened in the Streghe del Malocchio's underground cities."

That same anger that twisted deep in my belly earlier uncoils and winds through the rest of my body like a cobra ready to strike. I lean my head back against the cabinet and let the rage build, feel it stretching and creeping out from the spaces between my ribs. Pressing against my skin. Pulsing in time with my heartbeat. It snuffs out the tears. Smothers the sadness. Waits for my magic to reignite.

I wipe the tears away with an oily hand and carefully set Sinistro on the floor before rising to my feet. "I'm not going to be sad. We've got stuff to do."

Sinistro meows loudly, stretching as he kicks out his back feet. "A plan?"

"Yep. But first—" I open the refrigerator and pull out the rest of the tiramisu Rocco made for me, along with leftover garlic shrimp "—we eat."

I follow Sinistro into the dining room, and he hops onto the kitchen table, purring loudly as he takes small bites of shrimp. I dig into the glass dish of tiramisu and shovel a huge spoonful into my mouth. The strong coffee and sweet mascarpone fluff taste perfect together. Better, even, than the first piece. My stomach grumbles, and I realize it's been at least a day since I last had a real meal. I quickly eat more and rest back in my chair, closing my eyes and feeling the first sparks of magic come back to life.

Soon, the tiramisu and shrimp are gone. Sinistro licks some of the remaining mascarpone from the dish and twitches as it gets on his whiskers. The pulse of magic grows, catching in my core and slowly fanning out. I can feel Sinistro's magic, too, twirling across our bond and warming against mine. We're still not fully back to normal, but the vibration of it between us is promising.

We sit in silence, watching the sun rise over the blue sea. Less than a day left to save everyone. I get up and pour a large glass of ice water—and fill a bowl for Sinistro—before sitting back on my seat and quirking a brow. "If we're going to get the Streghe del Malocchio what they want, we're going to need more help," I say with a sigh. "A lot more help."

Sinistro takes a long drink of water and sits tall on the table, his tail flicking back and forth. "I have an idea. Though it's going to require the help, and convincing, of a few other magical creatures."

At his words, I feel my magic crackle against my skin. A smile crawls over my face. I lean in closer, whispering, "What do you have in mind?"

# 17

Trying to rest when your family and best friend are being held captive by a group of streghe that wants to eat their hearts isn't easy. It takes a few hours until I feel my magic vibrating in the space between my heart and belly. I extend my hand, feeling it travel down my arm and buzz in my fingertips. Sinistro stretches and hops down from his perch in the window frame. He flicks his tail through the air, and his magic smacks against mine.

"Andiamo! Time to put our plan in motion." I grab my backpack, already restocked with food, water, and ingredients. We rush through the front door to my garden.

Tartufo's tree shimmers with spider silk. Thousands and thousands of long, glistening, and strong threads of spider silk hang down from the tree's branches like fresh spaghetti.

"Tartufo!" I stand back, hands on hips, admiring my little friend's work. "You've outdone yourself. Thank you so much."

Tartufo's fuzzy brown head pops up from a low branch. His large eyes sparkle in the sunlight as he blinks out his response. I throw him a beetle, and he catches it, crunching down happily. Sinistro helps me arrange the sheets of sea serpent scales on the ground while I carefully collect the silk, laying it out on the scales and untangling the threads.

"We'll still need your help in Malafi crafting the web," I say, rolling up the scales and silk before gingerly tucking them into my backpack. "Are you okay to come with us?"

Tartufo blinks and leaps down onto my shoulder, fluttering his fluffy little legs against my cheek. I laugh at the tickle and gently pat him with a single finger. "You're a good friend, Tartufo."

"Come on, Giada." Sinistro nudges against my legs. "We still have a couple more things to do."

Nerves twist in my stomach as we run around the house, down the stairs, and into the backyard, ending up at its edge just before the path to our grotto. I lick my lips and hesitate, looking at Sinistro. "They're gonna say yes, right? They like me."

"You'll just need to convince them."

Nodding, I place my forefinger and thumb just inside my mouth and conjure a bit of my magic to amplify the sound. I whistle the tune Piccolina taught me, and it reverberates across the bright blue sea.

Nothing. The sky is clear, and the sun beats down on us.

"Maybe they didn't hear it?" Sinistro asks, squinting out at the horizon.

I wipe the sweat from my forehead and fidget with my ponytail. "Or maybe they don't want to come."

*Cawwww! Ca-caw, ca-cawwww!*

Papa Gryphon appears out of thin air, dropping his invisible shield as he comes to a graceful stop a few feet to our left. He shakes out his brown and white feathers, his long lion tail flicking back and forth as he looks at us.

"You made it!" I curtsy and Papa Gryphon bows his head.

With caution, I walk over to Papa Gryphon and run my

hands over his soft fur. My magic jolts up from my core and pulses in my fingertips. I tune in to Papa Gryphon's magic and feel him reach out in return. It's warm, receptive to mine. My heart beats faster. He still trusts me.

I touch the ends of his feathers, smiling. "Ciao, again. Thank you for coming."

His muscles twitch just under his skin, and, with my fingers, I trace along his shoulder blades where his fur meets bright white feathers. He's happy to be here and glad his daughter taught me the gryphon call. He's curious about what I need.

"We need your help with the Streghe del Malocchio." I concentrate my magic on communicating the request. He can't understand my words, but speaking the message aloud focuses it.

Papa Gryphon stiffens. He looks at me from the corner of his eye. Gryphons don't trust the Streghe del Malocchio. They're dangerous, and Papa Gryphon wants to be careful. He needs to protect his family and the other gryphons.

I swallow, toeing the dirt with my boot, and say, "They took my family and my best friend. If I don't give them a night sky, they'll eat their hearts. I need you to fly me up to the highest point in Malafi so I can hang the moon with spider silk until it's strong enough to float on its own."

*Caw-caww*. Papa Gryphon plucks at a few stray feathers. He feels bad about my family but still fears that drawing the Streghe del Malocchio's attention could endanger his pride.

"The plan is to sneak in before they even notice us and grab the moon. Tartufo is going to spin the web while we're flying, strap the moon to you, and then all we need to do is hang it from the highest root." I take a deep breath and look up into Papa Gryphon's eyes. "I won't let them hurt you or the other gryphons. I need my family back. You'd do anything for yours, yeah?"

Papa Gryphon tilts his head, holding my gaze. Finally, he nods his head. He'll do it. He'll help. I fling my arms around his neck and squeeze him in a hug.

"Oh, thank you, thank you, thank you!" I exclaim, releasing him. Papa Gryphon clicks his beak and ruffles his feathers.

Sinistro leaps onto a nearby rock. "Now we just need to get our stars."

"And a good thing is they can be found on the way to Malafi." I lead the way down the stairs to the grotto, Sinistro and Papa Gryphon not far behind. Tartufo crawls up my neck and onto my head, making a nest in my messy ponytail. The grotto glows its distinct emerald, and we duck down under the small entrance, hugging the wall as we go to avoid getting wet.

After a little bit, the grotto opens up more, and I can hear our boat rocking on the gentle waves. Rocco's moon beckoning supplies are still right where he left them the night he was taken. My stomach flips, but I clench my fists and push past the feeling.

"Ciao, lucciole," I call into the shadows. "It's me. Giada. Plus a few friends."

One by one the lucciole twinkle through the darkness. They circle around us, their glow so bright that soon the entire grotto is lit up as if I turned on a lamp. First, it's a couple hundred of them. But more and more flood into the space, darting through the air like shooting stars. Lucciole don't like the daytime. They hide in the grottos, only coming out around dusk. Their light doesn't have much competition at night, and lucciole love to show off their shine. Even better, unlike stars they won't die if they go underground.

A lucciole floats around my left ear before flitting between the curls of my ponytail. Another few dance atop Papa Gryphon's head. Their peacefulness radiates through the grotto, and a smile slips over my face. The fear over my family and Alessia being trapped in Malafi nearly slips from my mind. I shake my head. *Focus, Giada.*

"We need your help," I say.

The lucciole stop zooming around and hover in the air, as if they're all staring at me. I hold my hands in front of me, channeling my magic against theirs so they can better understand. It takes a moment to connect, but suddenly the full force of their soft, gentle magic washes over me and it becomes challenging to keep my arms up in the air. I fight back a yawn and press my message forward.

"There's a place where it's always night. You could be this village's stars. The streghe who live there would be in awe of you and your magic." The lucciole communicate through movement. Like synchronized swimmers, they flip through the air and swirl around the grotto in an intricate and choreographed dance. They're interested in this place. They know I speak of Malafi but have never ventured all the way down there.

"I can bring you there. Are you okay with living underground?"

The lucciole flicker their lights in harmony, joining to-gether in a sphere of light before fanning out and glow-ing as individual sparkles. They convey interest and are fine with living in the dark down below. As long as the Streghe del Malocchio adore them, they will provide a calming light rivaling that of the stars above.

"That's *exactly* what we need!" I clap my hands together, hopping up on my toes. "Thank you!" The lucciole dip down low, glittering in unison, as if bowing. I look at Sinistro, grin-ning. "I think this is going to work."

Sinistro watches as a lucciola weaves around his tail, saying, "I agree. Are you ready for phase two?"

I look at Papa Gryphon, the lucciole, and Sinistro. I run a finger over the top of Tartufo's head. "Phase two is of-ficially underway. It's time."

With a nod from Sinistro, I drop my backpack to the ground and pull out the scroll of sea serpent scales, un-furling it to reveal the long strands of spider silk. "Are you ready to weave these together, Tartufo? To bind them to Papa Gryphon's back?"

Tartufo blinks his eyes to say yes before scurrying down my arm and landing on the silk with a soft thud.

I press a hand to Papa Gryphon's side, reminding him

of our plan. He pushes against my magic in response and lies down on the ground so it's easier for Tartufo to reach him while Sinistro and I climb onto his back. Tartufo works fast and quickly builds a strong web from the strands of spider silk. Once we get one of the moons from the vine in Malafi, attaching it shouldn't be too hard, so long as none of the Streghe del Malocchio get in our way.

After a while, Tartufo finishes and clambers up Papa Gryphon's side and onto my shoulder. Sinistro squeezes in front of me, and I wrap my arms around him, holding on to Papa Gryphon's fur. With a deep breath, I guide him down the path that leads to under the world.

The piercing discordant violins greet us like an annoying friend. By now they don't even make my hair stand on end. They barely register as a headache. A sure sign I must be losing it after coming here three times.

We leave through Malafi's blue glowing grotto, and Papa Gryphon puts up his invisibility shield and unfurls his huge wings, leaping into the air and catapulting us into the pitch-black sky. Sinistro claws at my legs, and I hug him tighter. Behind us, the lucciole zip up into the darkness. But they don't glow. Not yet at least. Not until we get the moon settled in the tree root.

Glinting on the edge of the tallest cliff, next to the giant scales, is the moon vine. I gasp. Even from all the way up here, it's easy to see that the moons have grown even more since Sinistro and I left. They're the size of watermelons now and shining even brighter than before. I nudge Papa Gryphon, and he circles just above the trullo, getting lower and lower until the moon vine is only a couple yards above us.

Giving Sinistro a pat on his head, I carefully readjust so I'm facing the other way and holding on to where Tartufo attached his web to Papa Gryphon's back. The breeze from Papa Gryphon's wings pushes my curls against my face and freezes the sweat dripping down my neck.

A loud screeching cuts above the violins. I whip around, looking for the source of the noise. Papa Gryphon and Sinistro crane their heads, too.

*Caw-caw. Caww, cawwwww!*

*CAW! CAWWWWWW!*

A murder of crows—at least ten of them—launches off the top of Madre's trullo and hurtles toward us. Papa Gryphon stops his descent, and I fall face-first onto his neck, scrabbling at his fur to avoid slipping off.

"Ugh! These terrible birds."

The crows close the distance and take turns trying to peck at our heads. One of them pierces through the end of my ponytail, and I swat him away with my hand, his wing smacking me in the face.

"They're trying to knock us to the ground!" Sinistro yells, narrowly missing a crow's beak and ducking flat against Papa Gryphon's back.

"It's me! Giada!" I shout to the crows. "I'm trying to give the Streghe del Malocchio what they want." But they don't listen. They're intent on attacking Papa Gryphon.

He swerves away from two of the crows trying to poke his eyes, nearly bucking us off in the process. Blood rushes through my ears, and I swallow the fear that's lodged itself in my throat as I feel Papa Gryphon's invisible shield fall away. We're now exposed to any Streghe del Malocchio who look up. My palms vibrate as I communicate with him through our magic. "We need to work fast," I say. "The Streghe del Malocchio will know we're here." He nods and swoops down just as three of the crows dive after us.

He gets within a few feet of the moon vine, flapping his wings in an attempt to keep the crows from attacking. I squeeze my legs around his back so I don't fall and carefully extend my arms. My hands shake as I reach down and coax one of the moons from the vine. It floats up into my arms, nearly weightless. This moon's light isn't nearly as bright as the moon above Positano, but I still have to look away from it as I lay it in the center of the web.

Tartufo hops off my shoulder and quickly threads more strands of sticky silk to secure the moon. It should grow a little more, even after being plucked from the vine, and get to the size of a giant pumpkin over the course of a couple years. With the ingredients I added to encourage rapid growth, hopefully it won't take that long.

The webbing looks strong, and the moon's doing a better job of floating on its own than I thought it would. Tartufo hurries back up onto my shoulder, and I pat Papa Gryphon's back three times. "Andiamo," I call.

Papa Gryphon bursts through the air and twirls higher and higher up above the trulli. The crows aren't fast enough to catch us as Papa Gryphon pushes against his own top speeds, his muscles straining and fighting against him. I hold on tight as we near the sky's long, gnarled walnut tree

roots. Papa Gryphon's wings collide with some of the lanterns and send them careening into the sea below. Sitting
upright, I pull at the web and quickly wrap its ends to an
especially large and twisted root. The root groans under
the weight, but remains firm, the watermelon-sized moon
now shining down on Malafi. A rush of excitement swells
in my chest, and I throw my fists into the air.

"Lucciole!" Magic surges through me as I communicate
with the still-dark fireflies. "Time to shine as bright as the
stars."

Thousands of lucciole blink into view, and a quiet peace
falls over Malafi. Their light hums to life, glittering over the
village and stilling the cacophony of violins. For the first
time in probably forever, Malafi is quiet.

A smile widens on my face. The lucciole look just like the
stars. Their light even outshines the lanterns hanging in
the roots. They float in the air, completely at ease in their
new home. I press my hands to my lips, unable to keep
the happiness from bursting out of my body.

"We did it!" I shout. "It's magnifico!"

A prickle curls between my shoulder blades, and I look
down to see swarms of Streghe del Malocchio standing
out on the cliffs, down by the shore, in the middle of the

marketplace—thousands of them—staring up at us, the moon, and the lucciole. I press my lips into a firm line and twine my cornicello between my fingers before asking Papa Gryphon to fly back down to Madre's trullo.

Without warning, he swoops down, and Sinistro's pointy claws shoot into my arm. My ponytail flies back off my shoulders, the sweat on my brow drying in an instant. Papa Gryphon whooshes past the ruffled, irritated crows and makes a soft landing near the moon vine. Sinistro quickly hops down and shakes out his windswept fur. I follow after him and pat Papa Gryphon's side in thanks as he clicks his beak in return.

There's a faint slapping sound in the distance. I look over the cliff's edge, all the way down at the sea. Blinking, I rub my eyes to make sure I'm seeing what I think I am. "Sinistro! Look!"

He walks over and follows my gaze. Sinistro's tail coils into a question mark as he looks between me and the water. The sea's pushing and pulling against the shore, its edges soft with white foam. "The moon's creating a tide. It's really alive. Extraordinary!"

"We grew a real moon!" My gaze travels up to the night sky, and joy radiates out from my belly. The lucciole sparkle overhead, blinking just like the stars. And the moon shines down, bouncing off the white trulli and reflecting in the sea.

"That's powerful magic. You exceeded your end of the bargain." Sinistro rubs up against my legs. "Let's get Alessia and your family back."

I square my shoulders and tighten my ponytail, feeling the magic curling around my core. Tartufo crawls into my sweater pocket for safety as I march up to the trullo. "Ciao, Madre!" I yell while banging on the door. "Why aren't you out here with the rest of the streghe looking up at my hard work?" The door creaks open, and I nearly stumble through, fist extended to knock again. Gathering my courage, I hold my breath and walk into Madre's trullo, Sinistro at my heels.

The candelabra hanging overhead flares to life, and candlelight burns away the shadows, revealing a line of five golden cages, each one as lush and comfortable as Rocco's. The giant hourglass sits to the right, its bottom now filled with more golden sand than its top. But that doesn't matter now. I did what they asked.

All I see now are Rocco, Alessia, Mamma, Papa, and Zia Clementina locked away and frightened. They squint into the brightness as their eyes adjust to the light. Rocco looks the worst out of them all. My heart clenches. He looks even more disheveled than he did the last time I saw him.

"Giada?" Mamma exclaims. She presses her face to the bars and squeezes her arms out between them to reach for me. "Oh, Giada!"

"Mamma!" I take a few steps toward her cage, when a *click, click, click* stops me in my tracks.

Standing in the doorway of an emerald-and-ruby-zigzag-painted oval door to the left is Madre and the other streghe. She taps her cane against the tile again, the doll's blue eyes swiveling in their plastic sockets, a smile twisting on her face. Madre walks into the center of the room, her long black robes billowing out behind her, and the streghe follow.

I cross my arms over my chest to hide my shaking hands and plant my feet into the ground. My magic buzzes just underneath my skin, light and quick in my palms, ready to be used at a moment's notice.

"Well done, Giada," Madre says. She smooths out a stray hair on the side of one of her indigo ram's horns and gestures to the hourglass. "With time to spare, too."

"Let them go. Now." I stomp my foot and my magic crackles through my hair.

"Very well. You honored our bargain and now we'll do the same."

Pointing at the bits of gold and silver flashing on the cheese-making strega's neck, I add: "And give back Rocco and Alessia's cornicelli."

Madre arches an eyebrow and nods once. Before the cheese-making strega can react, the cornicelli float from her neck and land in my palm. Five crystal balls rise from the basket between the scales, twirling through the air before landing comfortably on the left scale. The scales resettle, balanced once more. Then, Madre raises her cane and slices it through the air. The cages groan open. Mamma pushes the door wider and runs for me.

"Mamma!" I yell just as she wraps me up in a hug, knocking the breath out of me. From over Mamma's shoulder, I see Papa helping Rocco out of his cage and Zia Clementina aiding Alessia. Mamma takes a step back and holds me in front of her. Tears stream down her cheeks, and she wipes at them with her fingers.

"My brave, sweet girl."

"How'd they capture you all?" I ask. "You, Papa, and Zia Clementina always wear your cornicelli!"

"There was salt and oil everywhere. The bad luck over-powered our protection wards—even our cornicelli." Mamma shakes her head. "We need to perform the Malocchio Prayer to rid the house of the evil eye."

"But it's over now. You're all safe."

"Yes, my darling." Mamma presses a hand to my cheek, and I close my eyes.

"Giada! Giada, you did it!" Alessia bounds toward us and throws an arm over my shoulders. "I'm so, so, so happy to see you!"

I hug Alessia tight. "I couldn't have done it without you."

Papa and Zia Clementina hold Rocco up between them. My throat tightens and lips quirk down as tears blur my vision. "Rocco!" I shout, my words choked.

Rocco raises his head, his tangled hair flopping over his eyes. He grimaces as Papa and Zia walk him over to us. "Giada." The three syllables come out slow, and his voice is rough, like the crunch of broken glass. But even though he's not one hundred percent, hearing him say my name—seeing him no longer trapped—is the best.

My grin widens, but I keep my distance, afraid to hug him in case I squeeze too tight. "Let's get home so we can res—"

*CAW, CA-CAWWWW!*

Papa Gryphon's pained cries cut through the trullo.

Before anyone can stop me, Sinistro and I rush through the front door in time to see three streghe struggling with Papa Gryphon. Golden chains are lashed over his body, pinning his wings to his sides. The smell of burning hangs in the air, as his feathers and fur are singed where they touch the gold chains. Gryphons are allergic to gold. He screeches again as he kicks and smacks at the streghe trying to keep him contained.

My magic surges forth from my core, and, without another thought, I channel it through my palms. I press my hands together, conjuring the light spell I use to see in the dark, only this time I focus all my rage into it and let the light heat up and become brighter than usual. When it becomes so hot that it sears my skin, I raise my hands in the streghe's direction. Beams of light blaze forth, and the streghe leap out of the way.

I hurry to Papa Gryphon and tug the heavy gold chains off his back, letting them clatter to the ground. Red welts cover his body, and blood pools by his wounds. He looks at me with pleading eyes and lets out a sad, pained screech.

"I'm so sorry." I press my hand to his face before slinging my backpack over my body and digging through it for supplies. A pit forms in my stomach as I look at just how deep his wounds go. How the blood seeps from them like rain rushing from a gutter. "I can fix you up, and you'll be good as new. Tartufo." I pull him from my pocket and set him on a nearby rock. "Do you have it in you to spin a bit more silk? It's an emergency."

Tartufo doesn't even take the time to blink. He looks up at Papa Gryphon and gets right to work spinning more silk for bandages. I pull my antichafing salve and the rest of the immortal jellyfish goo out of my backpack. It's not ideal, but they're the only ingredients I have on hand that can help. It was a bad move removing my first aid stuff earlier to fit all the moon-growing ingredients.

Groaning and whining, the three streghe struggle to their feet. They rub at their eyes and clutch their foreheads as they try to blink away the light I shone in their faces. With an angry huff, I turn on my heel and extend my arms to shield Papa Gryphon. "You're not taking him," I yell. "You can't keep taking and taking!"

"Giada?" Papa calls from near the trullo, his eyes panicked. "Are you hurt?" Everyone, including Madre and the other Streghe del Malocchio, has come outside to watch us.

"*I'm* not, but Papa Gryphon is." I toss my backpack to the ground and take off my sweater, pressing it to Papa Gryphon's cuts to clean up the bleeding. Throwing a glare at the three streghe standing on the opposite side, I add, "Why'd you hurt him? He's done nothing to you."

Madre swishes over in her billowing black robes. Her eyes are stone, jaw set as she looks at Papa Gryphon and me. I swallow, taking in her wrath, and am about to say something when she turns to face the three streghe and slams her cane down hard enough to crack the ground.

"Do you dare tip the scales without caution?" Madre's voice booms across the cliff side, her glare unwavering. "Do you dare go against our laws? This is not our way."

I toss my sweater, now drenched in blood, to the side and spread the immortal jellyfish goo over Papa Gryphon's open cuts. "I used this for Mamma Gryphon's injury," I murmur only so he can hear. "It's the best. Heals pretty much anything. We use it all the time."

"B-but, Madre," I hear one of the streghe plead, "we didn't have a choice. We need his feathers."

At this, I whip around and stare her down. "You can't just throw golden chains on a gryphon and take what you want. For one, they're severely allergic to gold. You could have killed him, and when a gryphon dies, its feathers and claws lose their magic. You would have gotten nothing." I grab the jar of antichafing salve and start rubbing it along the edges of Papa Gryphon's wounds. "Secondly," I call over my shoulder, "if you take a gryphon's feathers or snip their claws by force, the magic isn't as powerful. That's why it's critical to foster a relationship with them. Feathers and claw clippings given freely are the rarest and most potent." I put the jar away and turn to face the three streghe full on, hands on hips. "How dare you hurt him. You know nothing about creatures and think you're entitled to his magic. You're lucky I didn't throw more than just beams of light at you."

From my side, Madre stares down at me, eyebrow arched. "So much righteous fury for such a little girl. Impressive."

"Whatever," I shout, tossing my hands into the air. "You all can't take Papa Gryphon. Or any of the gryphons. Ever. Or else you'll have to deal with me again." I glare up at Madre. "And I know you wouldn't like that."

Madre tilts her head to the side, smiling. "You think I don't like you, Giada, but I quite enjoy your energy." She gestures to the three streghe and says, "I don't condone their actions. Not only have they hurt the creature, as you stated, they've also gone against the rules we must abide by as Streghe del Malocchio. He was not part of the initial bargain you and I agreed upon. Capturing him would tip the scales. It would cause disparity."

"Then why'd they do it? What's the point?"

"The Streghe del Malocchio have suffered without a moon and stars of their own. Living in darkness, even for hardy streghe like us, is no way to exist. Not all the time. Some covens are fine with it, and some even feast on the shadows. But the Streghe del Malocchio of Malafi…" Madre pauses, the smile dropping from her lips. She shakes her head. "We have grown weary and melancholy. Perhaps it's because we know of Positano up above. Of the sunshine and moon blessing the city each day and night. That could make it worse for us."

"And the Streghe del Malocchio wanted gryphon feathers and claws to help with that. Because you know these things can ease sorrow and restore a person's inner light." I shake my head. "Is that another reason you took Rocco?" I glance back at my parents and Zia Clementina. I don't want to tell Rocco's secret, but this is important. I softly add, "Because you knew about his tonic? How long were you watching him?"

"We had thought that if you failed and if we consumed his magic, we'd learn the secret of his tonic. But, since you succeeded, that's no longer a possibility." Madre picks a piece of lint off her robes, seemingly unbothered by how terrifying what she said sounds.

Snatching the spider silk Tartufo spun, I carefully lay it on the sea serpent scales. There's no time to create a bandage from the threads of silk, so the scales will just have to do as an alternative, holding the threads together. After placing the scales silk side down on the wounds, I turn back to Madre and the three streghe. "Why didn't you just ask for help? And not with weird messages like spilled salt and olive oil. Why didn't you talk to us?"

"The guaritori don't like us," Madre says.

"So what?" I roll my eyes, stomping a foot on the ground.

"We still would've helped you. We help *everyone*! Instead, your streghe tried to capture a gryphon and injured him in the process. And you kidnapped my brother! If you had only asked first, then maybe things would've been different." I rub a hand over Papa Gryphon's fur and gesture to the sky with the other. "Look what I did for you. You didn't have to take Rocco to ask for my help. No threats were necessary. I actually enjoyed growing that moon. I'm good at that."

Madre stares at the sky for a long time. Finally, she looks back down at me and says, "You're right, Giada. Though we strive for balance, our methods can be…" She taps a finger against the doll's head on her cane and grins. "Manipulative. *But*, because we like you, we'll be more forthright going forward."

"Ugh." I scrunch my nose. "You like me? I don't know if that's a good thing."

Madre's lips quirk as she twirls her cane through the air. "Since you're here and I am trying to learn—yes, even in my old age—is now a good time to ask if you could collect some gryphon feathers and claw clippings for us?"

I look back at my family and Alessia. At an exhausted

and hurting Rocco. It's possible he won't be too pleased later, especially since guaritori should never make deals with Streghe del Malocchio. And maybe I'm getting too comfortable around these strange streghe. But I'm technically still not a guaritrice, and sometimes bargains aren't so bad. "I have a better idea. If you promise to never *ever* kidnap another strega from up above, then maybe I can convince Rocco to regularly make some of his tonic for you."

Madre glances at Rocco before nodding. "Well, well, well, Giada. Striking a bargain?"

"Hopefully this one will be less traumatic," I remark.

"Like I said before, you'd make a good Strega del Malocchio if you wanted to."

"I've spent enough time underground, thanks. Plus, I couldn't pull off the fashion."

"Fair enough." Madre waves a hand. "Leave now and take care to watch for our messages from now on, Giada. This won't be the last you hear from us."

Madre and the other streghe on the cliff twirl on their toes and disappear in bursts of different-colored glitter. With no other reason to stay in Malafi, Sinistro and I lead everyone back above.

We exit through our grotto as the sun sets over the Mediterranean. Streaks of orange and pink kiss the dark blue sea, reflecting off the waves. Lucciole float out from the shadows, and their light joins in. Peace washes over us.

I squeeze Rocco's hand, and he looks down at me, a smile on his face.

# 18

Before we head home, we first take Alessia back to her family. Her mamma and papa wrap her up in huge hugs and kiss her all over her face, relieved that she is uninjured and, despite being missing for a full day, just tired and a little hungry. I promise Alessia I'll go over to her house tomorrow so we can discuss everything with her parents. Tonight, they just want to rest and spend time with her.

After that, we're all silent as we walk back to our house. Papa, Mamma, and Zia Clementina cast sideways glances at Sinistro every few steps. They don't seem to mind Papa Gryphon's presence, and that's likely because gryphons aren't signs of bad luck like black cats. But after everything with the Streghe del Malocchio, when it comes to bad luck, black cats like my familiar, Sinistro, are the least of my concerns.

Rocco and I think it's best for Papa Gryphon to stay with us for a couple days until he's fully healed and well enough to fly. Papa and Mamma don't argue with us, leading him into the downstairs room where they brew potions and store ingredients. I fix up Papa Gryphon's wounds with some additional ointments and salves, as well as with proper bandages. Mamma and Papa put down a couple blankets and bowls of food and water for him in the corner of the room. He circles around on top of them a few times before lying down and quickly falling asleep.

Finally, long after the sun dipped below the sea and the stars and moon began sparkling in the sky, we all sit down in the dining room to talk.

"So," Papa begins while placing a plate of salumi, melon, cheese, and bread on the table. "Your mamma and I go on a short trip, and you both get wrapped up with the Streghe del Malocchio." He rubs the graying hairs at his temple and shakes his head. "What on earth happened?"

Rocco looks at me from the corner of his eye. As soon

as we got home, he took a shower and put on a fresh pair of clothes. Not a complete cure, but already there's some color back in his face. He piles his plate with prosciutto, capicola, and Gorgonzola.

My stomach turns at the meats and cheeses, remembering the cheese-making strega's horrific sausages. With a sigh, I splay my hands out on the table and begin, "Well, for me, it started with some salt and olive oil."

"Some salt and olive oil?" Papa places his chin on his fists and waits for me to continue.

I walk them through everything that has happened these past few days, from finding Sinistro and realizing he's my familiar to climbing the cliff to ask the gryphons for help and seeing Rocco locked up. Tumbling from my mouth comes how I'm unsure about taking my guaritrice oath—especially now that I know Diana considers me one of her followers—and then I tell them about the bargain and my failed attempt to save Rocco. And, finally, I explain to them how Papa Gryphon and Tartufo helped me save everyone.

Silence. They all stare at me, blinking, mulling over my forty-five-minute explanation.

Papa opens his mouth and shuts it. Finally, he leans back

in his chair, arms crossed over his chest, and says, "You're uncertain about your oath." It's not a question. Out of *everything* I said, this is what Papa holds on to.

I scratch Sinistro's soft face and focus on his purrs, unable to look any of them in the face.

"Why are you worried about your oath?" Papa presses. Of course, even after the mess Rocco and I went through, he's going to zone in on this.

But now I've faced worse than his disappointment. Nails digging into my palms, I look up from Sinistro and meet Papa's gaze. "I don't feel a connection to Apollo," I state. "And I don't feel inspired by the work. People are tough for me."

Papa shifts in his seat like he wants to say something, but when Mamma and Zia both shoot him looks, he presses his lips together.

I continue, "But animals aren't. I'm good with them. My magic vibes with theirs. It's energized—more powerful— when I'm helping a gryphon or spider. That doesn't happen for me when I tend to humans. Look at Sinistro, for example." I nod to Sinistro, who is now lying sprawled across the table on his back, completely at ease in front of everyone. "He's my familiar. And I know guaritori don't have familiars. Only streghe Diana chooses as her own have them." I swallow, the next words stuck on my tongue. After a breath I find them, whispering, "Isn't that reason enough for me to follow her instead of Apollo?"

"I don't think this is right. Bellantuonos have been guaritori for hundreds of years. We're the most important of the fixers. We serve the people. For you to give all of that up?" Papa shakes his head.

Even though the Streghe del Malocchio were far scarier than Papa's disappointment, it still stings. I bite my lower lip to stop the tears from welling in my eyes and look down at the table, focusing instead on Sinistro's swishing tail. This is it. Papa will never let me do what I'm good at. Instead, it's all about silly tradition. I shouldn't be surprised.

"You know, I saw her in action, Papa," Rocco explains, his voice still scratchy. He takes a sip of his water before going on. "I thought it was a bad idea before. That she'd only curse herself if she didn't follow Apollo. But she's amazing when she's helping animals. Didn't you see her with that gryphon? A grown, male gryphon that would usually take off a person's arm for getting too close. And she was able to do it without even flinching. She can talk to them!" He grins and pops a piece of melon in his mouth.

"She even impressed the Streghe del Malocchio and made a successful bargain with them. That's nearly unheard of."

I stare at him, mouth agape. He turns to me, eyes softening. "You're not an embarrassment," he says. "And you never were. So what if you're not a guaritrice? You're a powerful and competent strega. One of the best I've ever seen."

Before I can stop myself, I throw my arms around him, the tears I was trying to hold back now racing down my cheeks.

"Ouch, easy," Rocco laughs. "Still dealing with some bruises."

"I love you so much. Thank you." I pull away from him and sit back down in my chair.

He ruffles my curls and laughs, "You saved my life. The least I can do is talk you up a little."

"Even so," Papa says, holding up a hand. "Leaving a god is dangerous. You mentioned your fears that Giada would curse herself if she left Apollo." He looks at me, frowning. "I don't want you to lead a life fraught with bad luck for choosing to follow a different god."

"But how can it be bad to honor Diana and care for animals?" I press my hands onto the table, nearly bursting

**293**

out of my seat. "Nonna took good care of the creatures in her garden and grew so many beautiful and rare plants that benefited our family and other guaritori. She didn't take the traditional path and led a good life."

"I can't worry for my daughter's well-being?" Papa asks. "I don't want you to suffer."

"She'll suffer if she can't do what she loves. What she's good at," Zia Clementina asserts. She sits at the far edge of the table, idly running a hand down Sinistro's back. Papa turns to her, frowning. My stomach flops. Zia's been quiet this whole time, and whenever she and Papa get on this particular topic, it usually ends with her storming from the house and them not talking for months.

Zia Clementina looks up from Sinistro and into her brother's eyes. "Remember when we were kids? How easy it was for you to pick up the guaritore magic, fixing people in no time at all. Loving schooling at the Torre di Apollo and learning all the spell work and potions?" She shakes her head, hands fisted in front of her. "You know it wasn't like that for me. I couldn't cast a simple suturing spell. I couldn't even mend a skinned knee. My magic felt tense and uncomfortable. It didn't feel right.

"I didn't know myself until I discovered I was an oracle.

**294**

Flipping through tarot cards, scrying, channeling from the other side—doing these things was like waking up for the first time. I wasn't a failure like I thought I was when trying to be a guaritrice. My magic flowed freely. It felt good. *I* felt good." She takes a deep breath and presses her fingers to her cornicello. "Traditions are meant to evolve. If we all stayed put and kept repeating the same things as our ancestors, we'd get nowhere. New ideas aren't a bad thing, nor are they harbingers of ill fortune."

Papa stares at Zia Clementina for a moment before reaching out and placing a hand on hers. She looks up sharply, confusion in her eyes.

"You never told me how difficult it was to be a guaritrice," Papa says. "I thought it was your rebellious streak."

A smile slides over Zia Clementina's lips. "Maybe that was part of it, too."

"I'm sorry you had such a hard time." Papa's eyes are glassy with tears. He presses his thumb and forefinger to his eyes and scrubs them away. "I never made it easy for you. Never listened when you told me you were hurting. I was only afraid for you. All I could think of was the bad luck you were bringing upon yourself. Instead of listening, I let that fear dictate how I treated you. I'm sorry for that."

"We have a lot of lost time to make up for." Zia squeezes Papa's hand and wipes away her own tears. She shakes her head. "Don't make the same mistake with your daughter."

Mamma smiles at Papa and Zia before turning to me, saying, "Giada, we don't want you sacrificing your happiness for tradition." She eyes Papa, arching a brow at him and tilting her chin in my direction.

"Your mamma's right," he begins. Papa drums his fingers against the table and sighs. "I may not fully understand your choice, but I'll support you no matter what. As long as you're absolutely sure that following Diana is what you want."

I lean over the table, heart bursting out of my chest. "Absolutely! It's the only thing I want in this entire world."

"You know…healing animals isn't all that different from healing people," Mamma muses, tilting her head. "And Diana and Apollo are siblings. Complementary, even— the sun and the moon." She exchanges a look with Papa. "I wonder if the Guaritore Council would agree to letting followers of Diana, those who use their magic to help animals, take the oath and be considered a different kind of guaritore. After all, Diana's followers are still fixers. Like magical gardeners or builders."

"The council will be convening soon. Christmas Eve and the oath ceremony are fast approaching, too," Papa says. He looks to me and smiles. "You don't have to take your oath this year. Let me convince the council to admit followers of Diana into the fold. If they agree, then we can talk about you taking your oath. But until then, let's wait."

"This is, like, the best birthday present ever!" I jump from my chair, pick Sinistro up, and twirl us around the room.

Rocco rolls his eyes. "It's not your birthday yet."

"Whatever. An *early* birthday present."

"But…" Papa continues.

I stop dancing, and Sinistro leaps from my arms, curling up on my warm seat. "Uh-oh. What is it?"

"Since you'll still be turning thirteen in a couple days, I still think it's best for you to take on your apprenticeship. I have a family in mind. A good family who isn't as traditional as typical guaritori." He strokes his chin and looks at me with warmth in his eyes. "You remember the Calamoneri family, right? They visited a few summers back."

I nod. "Moss is my pen pal. We still write letters to each other every now and then."

"They'll take good care of you and help foster your gifts."

"But they live all the way in New Jersey." Panic edges my words. It's too far away from home. From Mamma, Papa, Rocco, and Zia Clementina. "What am *I* gonna do in New Jersey?"

"You're going to become the best magical veterinarian the world has ever seen," Papa says.

I squint at him, arms crossed over my chest. "What if I get homesick? What if I don't like the way their house smells or how Mrs. Calamoneri makes her Bolognese?"

"Give it a chance," Mamma says. "We can visit so you don't get lonely."

"The apprenticeship will be good for you, Giada." Rocco smiles. "You'll learn a thing or two."

"Maybe…" I say.

I look at my family. At each one of them, their support and love almost overwhelming. As powerful as any kind of magic. They may not understand completely, but that's not stopping them from encouraging me.

"Ugh. Fine. I'll go to New Jersey." I try to sound put out by the decision, but I can't keep the excitement from my voice. Magic buzzes just under my skin. It's a little scary thinking about going to live somewhere else for a whole year without my family, but they've got my back.

I'm not a disappointment. Or an embarrassment.

I'm Giada Bellantuono, and I will be the best magical veterinarian the world has ever seen.

* * * * *

# ACKNOWLEDGMENTS

This book wouldn't be what it is without my fabulous editor, Connolly Bottum. Thank you so much for all you've done to help bring Giada to life. I'd also like to thank Gigi Lau and Devin Elle Kurtz for capturing Giada, Sinistro, and their gryphon friend so beautifully. Thank you to Carla DeSantis for making sure I stayed true to the Italian language and culture. And another big thank-you to Bess Braswell for being as excited about Giada and her friends as I am. Working with Inkyard has been a true gift and I am so lucky to have you all.

Thank you Dhonielle Clayton, Clay Morrell, and all of

Cake Creative. Dhonielle, you are a true light and bring so much goodness to my life. I am so honored to continue working with you and to have you as a mentor and friend. And thank you Jo Volpe, Jenniea Carter, Suzie Townsend, and Sophia M. Ramos, as well as everyone at New Leaf Literary. You believed in Giada and in me, for which I am incredibly grateful.

To my dad, John Cannistra, and my sisters, Andrea and Allyson. I would save all of you from scary streghe if I needed to. I love you all so much. And to my wonderful husband, Dan, who patiently listens to me ramble about Giada's adventures and will read my writing to let me know if it's good (or bad). You are my Tabitha.

And, finally, a huge thank-you to all who read Giada's story and love her. I hope, like Giada, you all have marvelous adventures. But hopefully ones that aren't as scary.